## ABOUT THIS BOOK

*Welcome to Havenwood Falls, a small town in the majestic mountains of Colorado. A town where legacies began centuries ago, bloodlines run deep, and dark secrets abound. A town where nobody is what you think, where truths pose as lies, and where myths blend with reality. A place where everyone has a story. Including the high schoolers. This is only but one . . .*

With her raven-black hair, porcelain-white skin, and shy demeanor, Zoey Mills has been the target of bullies since childhood, no matter how many times her family moved. She expects nothing to change when they relocate to Havenwood Falls, her parents' hometown. What she doesn't expect is to discover that she inherited her eccentricities—as the next generation of a long line of frost dragons.

As she learns to accept she's on the cusp of becoming a shifter, she finds out her new best friend isn't human, either. But the boy Zoey's fallen for is, earning the disapproval of her grandfather and patriarch and fueling the fire of a decades-long feud among her extended family. Elitism and prejudice take on whole new meanings.

While she wants to trust her instincts and follow her heart, Zoey discovers that hiding who she really is and playing by the rules would make life a lot simpler. But simple doesn't mean easy. She must find her strength somewhere within and embrace her destiny—or risk losing everyone she cares about. And all of this on the eve of her Sweet Sixteen.

# SOMEWHERE WITHIN

## A HAVENWOOD FALLS HIGH NOVELLA

## AMY HALE

# HAVENWOOD FALLS HIGH BOOKS

*Written in the Stars* by Kallie Ross

*Reawakened* by Morgan Wylie

*The Fall* by Kristen Yard

*Somewhere Within* by Amy Hale

*Awaken the Soul* by Michele G. Miller

*Bound by Shadows* by Cameo Renae

*Fata Morgana* by E.J. Fechenda

*Forever Emeline* by Katie M. John

*Reclamation* by AnnaLisa Grant

*Avenoir* by Daniele Lanzarotta

*Avenge the Heart* by Michele G. Miller

*Curse the Night* by R.K. Ryals

*Blood & Iron* by Amy Hale

*Shadows & Spells* by Cameo Renae

*Falling Deep* by J.L. Weil

*Saving Infiniti* by Rose Garcia

*Willful* by Liz Ferry

*Cast in Moonlight* by Ali Winters

*Promise the Moon* by Kallie Ross

*Blurred Lines* by Daniele Lanzarotta

*Ascending Darkness* by J.L. Weil

*Finding Infiniti* by Rose Garcia

*Unicorn's Lament* by Megan Linski

*Paper Bird* by Amy Richie

*Predestined* by Valia Lind

*Rediscovered* by Morgan Wylie

*Ashes of Fate* by Apryl Baker

Stay up to date at <u>www.HavenwoodFalls.com</u>

## OTHER BOOKS BY AMY HALE

*Ulterior Motives*

THE SHADOWS TRILOGY
*Shadows of Jane*
*Shadows of Deception*
*Shadows of Deliverance*

*Catching Whitney*

*Letters From Jayson*

*For all the young people who fight to be normal.*

*Normal is boing and overrated.*
*Be unique.*
*Aim for extraordinary.*
*Show the world why it's great to be you.*

# CHAPTER 1

*I* glanced at the boxes still waiting to be unpacked as I attempted to relax in my new bedroom. The excitement that generally accompanied a new house was missing. I felt like we moved more than we stayed still. My dad had assured me this would be the last time, and while I thought he believed that to be true, I had my reservations.

My first memories of moving took place at age seven. I don't remember all the details, but I do recall a loud commotion, after which Mom had run out to the backyard to get me. She rushed me into the car, and we left. Just like that. No goodbyes to the neighbors. No "grab a few things for overnight." We just left. Two days later, my dad arrived at our hotel room, two states away, driving a moving truck containing all our belongings. At the time, I was afraid to ask what happened, but it had certainly crossed my mind with every successive move. I'd had an unpleasant sensation down in my gut each time I attempted to mention the subject, so I'd always chickened out.

So there I was, on move . . . what was it? Move eight? Yeah, I thought this was move number eight. One would think I'd be used to starting over, and over, and over. But the truth was that with every packed box, I felt like I'd left a part of me behind. Even if that part wasn't important, it was a segment of my scattered life that no longer felt valid. Those memories now lived in the past.

This latest move had been prompted by a family member. It turned out I had a grandfather here in Havenwood Falls, Colorado. My parents had never talked about him before, so I'd assumed my dad didn't know who his father was. It was the only logical explanation for never hearing about Grandpa Mills. You couldn't talk about someone you didn't know, right?

My parents had received a letter that my grandfather, Lawrence Mills, had become very ill, and was possibly dying. Mom and Dad seemed frustrated by the phone conversations they'd had with him afterward. Ultimately, I held the impression they'd decided it was time to mend fences. Granted, they'd never told me what busted the fences to begin with, but maybe someday I'd learn all the deep, dirty family secrets. All families had a skeleton or two in their closets, so I'd heard. I suspected my family to be no different.

I stood and opened the box closest to my bed. It contained some of my clothes and the most beautiful jewelry box I'd ever seen. It'd been a gift from my parents for my sixteenth birthday. I hadn't actually had that birthday yet, but it was only about a month away. Dad had said that he wanted to give it to me before the move. "Something special for your new room," he'd said. I thought he'd been attempting to bribe me so I wouldn't complain about changing houses and schools yet again. It kinda worked.

I ran my fingers over the smooth metal casing, and I could almost feel it vibrate beneath my fingers. I didn't know how to explain it, but it felt as if the box itself was alive. Every time I touched it, I felt a zing of positive energy pulse through me. No doubt these sensations all took place in my mind, but I allowed myself to indulge the fantasy just the same. As long as I didn't say it out loud, I should be safe. Admitting it to others would have been like saying I'd grown a third leg, but no one could see it.

I placed the gold box on my nightstand and studied the intricate design on the lid, which looked much like a maze, with lines darting out from the center in odd geometric patterns. From the moment I laid eyes on it, I'd tried to figure out if there were some kind of labyrinth hidden in all the chaos, but if so, I had yet to solve it.

Regardless, it was another great addition to what my mother lovingly called my "jewelry hoard." I did have a slight obsession with jewelry, but really, what teenage girl didn't? I wouldn't call it a hoard.

"Zoey, here's another box with your name on it." Dad pushed through my bedroom door and set the box on the bed beside me. "Sheesh, that's heavy. What do you have in there? Anvils?"

I rolled my eyes at him. "Yes, Father. I have an anvil addiction. You've found me out."

He smirked. "So much sass in such a little person."

I reached over and pulled the tape from the top of the box, then glanced inside. "Oh," I said.

Dad simply raised his eyebrows in curiosity.

"It's my jewelry boxes," I said quietly.

His soft laughter followed him to the door, and he sent me a wink. "Enjoy." He walked out of the room and gently closed the door behind him.

I looked into the box again. I had several jewelry boxes, most of them very full. *Okay, maybe I do have a jewelry-hoarding issue. Is there a therapy for that?*

AFTER LUNCH, Dad had some things to take care of at his new job running Simple Treasures Pawn Shop, so that left just Mom and me cleaning and unpacking in the kitchen.

Mom crossed her arms and leaned against the tan Formica counter. "What do you say we run into town for coffee? A latte sounds great, and I noticed a nice-looking shop as we drove through town."

I put away the last plate in the stack I'd unpacked and wiped my hands on my jeans. "Sure. Sounds good."

She smiled at me. "Perfect. As much as I love this new house, I'm eager to get out for a few minutes."

I didn't comment. I knew she wanted to hear me gush about the new place. After all, it was a nice house. A relatively new brick ranch house, it contained three bedrooms and loads of extra space. My bedroom easily overshadowed the dimensions of any other room I'd ever had. I even had my own bathroom. The pale yellow walls and white gauzy curtains gave my room a cheery feel. My white bedroom suite fit perfectly within the space. Much to my mother's delight, there were hardwood floors throughout. All I could think about was how cold those floors would be first thing in the morning. I made myself a mental note to ask for a rug in my bedroom.

The main part of the house had an open floor plan with the living room, kitchen, and dining room all in one large area. The fireplace had to be my favorite feature of the house, aside from my bedroom. The large grate could hold a decent-sized load of wood, and I could imagine the relaxing crackle as the flames warmed my fingers and toes while the smell of the fire saturated my clothes.

I had every reason to love our new home, yet all I could muster for my mother was a less-than-excited smile. As for the town—it was lovely. The gorgeous mountains surrounding the town boxed us in and lent a cozy, protected feel. As it was November, the air felt frigid and crisp, but also clean. Air this fresh was foreign to me, since all our other homes were in larger cities filled with smog and the various odors that accompanied living in a crowded area with several thousand people. One apartment had been so poorly located that a few times I wondered if I'd ever get the stench of garbage out of my nostrils. There was nothing like living a few blocks from a landfill when the wind blew just right. Thankfully, that stay was short-lived.

Havenwood Falls was perfectly sized for exploring. I hadn't had a chance to look everything over yet, but Mom assured me I could easily walk from one end of town to the other. Since I'd always felt pulled to the outdoors, I should have been thrilled, but moving and leaving what little stability we'd had dampened my spirits. The unknown was always scary. I'd never been good with change.

Mom pushed away from the counter. "C'mon, kiddo. Let's get some caffeine."

She wasn't kidding about the size of Havenwood Falls. We'd only been on the road a few minutes when we pulled into a spot in front of a collection of cute little storefronts on the town square. We stepped onto the sidewalk, and I glanced at the surrounding businesses. It seemed to be the typical small-town America kind of place, except for a few eclectic shops, which oddly didn't seem out of place. I spotted Madame Tahini's, whose sign advertised potions, palm readings, and other services. I couldn't say I'd ever been in a store like that. It intrigued me. It was at the end of the block, next to Simple Treasures Pawn Shop, which was owned by my grandfather and now managed by my dad.

Directly in front of our parking space was Coffee Haven. The bell over the door greeted us with the light tinkle of chimes as we entered the shop. The scent of coffee and baked goods hit me immediately. I was suddenly thankful for the distraction and the promise of chocolate. I wasn't as into the whole froufrou drink thing as my mom was. If it had a weird name and complicated list of ingredients, she'd try it. I honestly preferred hot cocoa over coffee. Thankfully, most coffee places offered both. With it being the first week in November, the weather was perfect for a warm drink.

I glanced around the cozy space, and my eyes were instantly drawn to a section near the back of the shop. Shiny silver, copper, and gold hung from various displays, and the overhead lights caused a sparkle from the beads and gems as I moved to the right or left. My quest for hot chocolate was all but forgotten.

"I see that look in your eye," Mom teased.

"What?" I shrugged. "I'm just looking around."

"Well, why don't you go look closer, and I'll order your drink. You want your usual? With peppermint?" She asked.

"Yeah, that'd be great. Thanks." I wasted no time in getting to the jewelry display. Several gorgeous pieces were front and center, and I couldn't help but reach out and touch them. I had an affinity for all jewelry, but these were expertly handcrafted by someone named Serena Alverson, and I found myself wishing I had such a creative gift. Of course, if I did, I'd likely end up with more jewelry than all the stores in town combined, so it was probably fortunate I didn't possess that talent.

I glanced down at the bracelet hanging from my wrist. It was my favorite, and my parents had gifted it to me on my tenth birthday. The green and yellow crystal beads were strung together on a delicate gold chain. Inside the gift box there had been a note indicating that the crystals were fluorite and yellow jasper, providing the dual function of an energy shield and a protective amulet. I wasn't sure I bought into all that, but I loved wearing it just the same.

"Zoey, here's your drink." My mom's voice pulled me from the allure of shiny objects, and she motioned for me to join her at a small table near the large picture window in front. My mother and I were opposites. Her short brown hair barely reached her shoulders, and her eye color matched it perfectly. Naturally petite, she possessed an inner grace and beauty. She preferred more casual clothing, but no matter what she wore, she made it look classy. She oozed charm and confidence. I did not. I was more comfortable reading in my room than I was socializing. Outside of us both having pale complexions and being short, I appeared to be nothing like her—a disappointing realization.

My dad was a tall man, easily over six feet in height with only a slightly darker skin tone and a muscular build. His hair had a thick texture with waves, and while dark, it was nowhere near the raven black of my own hair. His eyes were blue, where mine were gray with hints of blue. His self-assurance inspired me, and I had idolized him for as long as I could remember. He was my hero. I seemed so very different from them both. I often wondered if, upon my eighteenth birthday, they'd tell me I was adopted. It wouldn't have surprised me.

I took a seat opposite my mother and cupped the warm mug in my hands as I sipped it cautiously. Perfect. I looked up at the counter and noticed the young woman behind it smiling at me. Her name tag said Willow. *Such a pretty name!* I gave her a thumbs up to indicate my pleasure, and she winked at me, then turned to wipe down one of the espresso machines.

"So, what did you think of the jewelry? Anything you can't live without?" my mom asked as I took another careful sip of my drink.

"There are a few that are amazing, but I should probably at least get my room unpacked before I start adding more to my collection." I thought back to the various jewelry boxes in my room still waiting for my attention.

She laughed and reached across to pat my arm. Bad timing on her part, or on mine. As she moved, so did I—I scooted my mug to the side, directly in her path. Her fingers hit the cup and tipped it over, spilling the scalding hot contents all over my right hand.

I yelped in pain, and my mom jumped up to help me. Willow appeared at our side quickly, and I vaguely remembered hearing her ask how she could help. My instinct was to blow on the back of my hand, and to my amazement, impossibly cool air passed over my lips and cooled my skin. I watched in shock, and honestly some horror, as ice crystals formed over the burned area.

My mom wrapped her arms around me, shielding my hand and face from the view of those around us. A towel was thrust between our heads by a tight-smiled Willow.

"I've got this. Go take care of her before anyone notices." Willow's voice barely registered above a whisper.

She and my mom exchanged a look that I couldn't understand, then Mom nodded and ushered me out the door.

"It's okay, baby. Let's get you to the hospital to have that looked at." Mom spoke louder than necessary, and I began to think I was losing my mind—or dreaming.

The pain had disappeared, and I had a morbid eagerness to peek under the dish towel to see how bad my injury really was. I glanced back into the shop and saw Willow quickly cleaning up the mess we'd left behind.

It seemed like only seconds before I found myself sitting in the passenger seat as Mom backed out of her parking space.

I peeled the towel back from my hand, expecting to either see the worst, or see that I'd imagined the severe burn, but found nothing but a small mark. What I didn't expect to see . . . I didn't even know what it was. It was white, shimmery, and hard—almost like a shell.

Panic welled up in my chest. I struggled to breathe.

"Mom?" I could hear the fear in my own voice, so I knew she heard it too.

"It's okay, sweetheart. It's gonna be fine." She pulled out her cell phone and hit a button. "Call Tristan," she said loudly.

The phone answered back, "Calling Tristan Mills."

Mom put the phone to her ear and waited only a few seconds, then said, "Tristan, it's happening. Meet us at home as soon as you can."

I heard the muffled voice of my dad say, "On my way," and then the line went dead.

"Mom?" I asked again. "What is this? What's happening?"

She glanced at me and sighed a deep, worried-sounding breath. "It's a long story. Dad and I will explain it all when we get home."

We drove in silence until we reached our new house—not the hospital, by the way. My gut told me something big loomed before me. Something I was totally unprepared for.

# CHAPTER 2

*W*e pulled into our driveway just seconds before Dad arrived in his black Toyota RAV4. He ran to the door and unlocked it, then waved us inside as quickly as possible. I worried about the cool air and the weird burn, but I was even more concerned by the way my parents reacted.

Once inside, Mom sat me on the sofa between her and Dad. She gently grasped my wrist and flashed me a reassuring smile. "We need to show your father."

I looked at my hand, then back up at her, and felt the previously unshed tears start to roll down my face.

"It's okay, sweetheart. Let me see," Dad said with a calm assurance he hadn't previously displayed. He pushed up the sleeves of his red sweater and held out his hand.

I removed the towel and gingerly placed my hand in his. He frowned and closed his eyes. "Well, I guess that settles it."

Mom nodded. "Yeah, it does."

I grew annoyed at all the completely unhelpful answers. "Settles *what*? You guys are scaring me!"

Mom grasped my left hand as Dad continued to hold on to my right. He gave my fingers a tight squeeze. "We aren't like other families."

I rolled my eyes at that. "No duh. I've known that for a long time. What does that have to do with this freaky scab on my hand?"

Mom slipped her other arm behind me and around my shoulder. "No, sweetheart, you aren't understanding your dad. Just give him a few minutes to explain."

"We are different because we aren't completely human. We're called shifters. Our specific species is dragon—frost dragon to be exact." Dad's demeanor was as if what he'd just told me wasn't completely bonkers. He acted like he'd just announced he'd taken a new job or something.

"Dragons?" The high pitch of my voice gave away my lack of emotional control.

"Sweetheart," my mom said. "Stay calm."

"Calm?" I screeched. "What the hell? How can we be dragons? We are people! Shifters, or whatever you called it, aren't real!"

Mom frowned at my use of the word hell, but at that point, I wasn't worried about dropping a dollar in the swear jar. Crap, I'd have been happy to dump my entire life savings in there if it would have allowed me to truly express how I felt at that moment.

"Dragons?" I repeated. "Huge, lizardish, winged creatures? That kind of dragon? How is this even possible? You're joking, right? Please say you're joking!"

Dad ran a finger over my weird scab. "This is a scale. It's a method of protection for us. Like armor." He glanced at my mom.

Mom frowned. "I accidentally knocked hot chocolate on her hand. She blew on the burn and . . . well . . ."

"Ah," said my dad, as if that cleared this entire enigma up.

I stood and paced in front of them. "Why do I have a scale?"

Mom spoke again. "Your natural instinct was to blow on your burn, as most would do, but unlike most, your inner dragon kicked into protection mode and blew frigid air out to stop the burn. Then it formed a scale to protect the skin until it's fully healed." She sounded a little in awe by this process.

I held up both hands. "Wait a minute. How come I'm just now learning about this?"

"Well," Dad said as he leaned back on the sofa, "if you possess the gene, it's triggered around your sixteenth birthday. You're only a few weeks away from that. Now that we know for sure you possess that gene, we can prepare you for what to expect next."

"Next?" I gulped. That sounded ominous.

"It's kind of like going through puberty." Mom smiled. "You'll notice minor changes up to your sixteenth birthday, when the gene is fully developed. What those changes will be? We can only guess. Everyone is different."

"Fully developed? What does that mean? Will I become a huge creature or something?" I could feel myself begin to hyperventilate.

"It's not quite like that. It's more—" Dad was interrupted by the doorbell. "Hold that thought." He ran to answer the door.

Mom motioned for me to join her again on the sofa. I sat next to her and stared at the scale on my hand.

Dad re-entered the room moments later. He clutched a letter between his fingers, his face solemn.

"What is it?" Mom asked.

"It's from my father. He'd like us to join him for dinner tonight." Dad didn't look pleased, which confused me. *Isn't Grandpa the reason we moved here to begin with?*

Mom nodded, but also appeared disturbed by the idea.

Dad sighed and looked at me. "I'm sure you'll learn more tonight, but I'll give you the summary. We come from an old line of frost dragons that originated in Iceland. Your Grandpa Mills is the patriarch of our family. Grandma Mills passed away before you were born. Everyone in my family has the shifter gene." He glanced at Mom. "Your mother is human, so there had always been the possibility that the gene would skip you."

I looked at my hand once again. "So I'm half human and half dragon?"

"More or less." Mom gave my shoulders a squeeze.

"I can't believe I'm hearing this. It's crazy," I muttered.

"It gets crazier," replied Dad. "Your great-grandfather settled in Havenwood Falls as one of the original founders of the town. This place came to be because supernatural beings from all over needed a safe place to live."

My eyes widened. "So there are other dragons here?"

"Other frost dragons? Outside of our family, none that I'm aware of, but there are other dragons, as well as witches, werewolves, vampires, fae, ghosts . . ." His voice trailed off when he noticed I was getting the point.

"Ho-ly crap." I couldn't believe what I heard. "All those things in fairy tales and horror stories are real?"

"Yes, but don't believe everything you read. Not all supernatural creatures are bad. In fact, many just want to be left to live in peace. Again, this is why Havenwood Falls is perfect for us." His eyes were full of emotion that bordered on pain, but something else lurked there too. Sadness? Longing? I wasn't sure.

"So why have you never mentioned Grandpa before?" I had to know why they kept all this from me for so long, especially since there was a possibility this secret would be life-changing for me.

"Havenwood Falls is protected by a memory ward. Once you leave, it's only a matter of time before you forget it exists. I think the memories were hidden somewhere in our minds, including your grandpa, but for the most part, we simply forgot." His shoulders were tense, and I sensed his discomfort.

"There's more to this story, isn't there? With Grandpa?"

"Yes," he stated. "But we'll have to continue this discussion later. I have to take care of some things before dinner tonight."

I opened my mouth to protest, but he held up one hand to stop me. "I promise you'll be told all the details. It'll just have to wait a bit longer. You have the bulk of the information you need for now."

I turned to my mom. "We live in a town full of supernatural creatures."

She nodded.

"How do all the regular people in town deal with that?" I could imagine the terror the human townspeople must have felt upon learning something so bizarre.

"Well," Mom sighed. "Most of the humans in town don't know about the supernatural beings that live here. This is a secret. One you need to be very careful with."

*How am I supposed to pretend all is normal when I have this huge secret?*

"Wait, what about Willow? From the coffee place?" I remembered how she jumped right in to help. She and my mom working in tandem.

"Willow is fae," Mom stated in a matter-of-fact tone.

"Fae," I repeated. "She looks so human."

"Faerie glamour. It helps them blend in, just as you do as a shifter. No humans will ever know you're a dragon, unless you tell them or they see you in that form."

The memory of that first, frantic move came rushing back. "When we moved, when I was seven. What happened? Why did we act like we were escaping something?"

Mom closed her eyes. "Dragons are territorial." She smiled at my dad a moment before turning back to me. "Understandably, human men are, too. Your father came home and found our neighbor trying to touch me. I was fighting him off, but I wasn't winning. Dad shifted in the backyard, and the other guy peed himself before passing out. We couldn't safely stay there after that." She squeezed my hand. "I'm sorry we've had to move so much. The other moves were job-related, with a touch of restlessness. I think we missed Havenwood Falls and didn't even realize it."

Mom brushed the hair back from my face and kissed my temple. "Now, we'll put a bandage over that scale so no one will see it, then you need to get some rest. You're going to need it for tonight."

*Great, more cryptic talk that tells me nothing.* "Is something bad happening tonight?" I mustered the bravery to ask.

"Not if I can help it." Dad's face grew stern, and I knew that asking more questions right now would only be met with silence.

I spent the better part of my afternoon online, looking for anything relating to dragons in Iceland. To my frustration, I didn't find much, and what I did find was based on video games or something similar, so I had no confidence the information could be trusted. I also searched for dragons in general, but there were many various sources, all giving conflicting information. I was frustrated and scared. Mom and Dad seemed perfectly cool with it all, but then, they'd had decades to adjust. Or maybe more. I realized then that I didn't know exactly how old my dad was. We had birthdays, and his age had been mentioned, but he still looked much like he did in my kindergarten days. I had always assumed that good genes were responsible. I obviously wasn't far from the mark, except that there weren't human genes involved.

I searched until my eyes burned, then slammed my laptop closed in frustration. I'd considered talking to Mom about it more, but I had yet to address how I felt about them keeping this from me. I acknowledged the sense of betrayal, even if they did have a good reason. I rested my head on my pillow and tried not to think about anything. It seemed a better option than losing my mind. I closed my eyes and inhaled, trying to relax.

When I opened my eyes, darkness greeted me. My vision adjusted, and my room resembled a jail cell. I rubbed my face, trying to shake off the dream I knew I was having. It didn't work. I rolled off the small bed and walked to the bars.

"Hey! Is anybody there?" I yelled at the top of my voice.

A man walked out of the darkness and sneered at me. "Quiet!"

"Sir, please. Let me out." I tried not to cry.

"We don't let monsters roam free." His caustic tone and expression of disgust terrified me as he stepped closer.

"Me?" I asked. "I'm not a monster. I'm just a girl."

"No. You're the worst kind of monster imaginable." He reached through the bars and started to strangle me.

I fought back with all my might, but couldn't break free of his grasp. A roar ripped from my lips, and in an instant, I was looking down on the man from a great height. Fear filled his eyes, and I roared again, then bent my head down and ate him with one bite.

I woke up drenched in sweat from the nightmare. It turned out I did take a short nap, and I was surprised at just how exhausted I really was. I guess finding out you're part dragon will do that, with the obvious addition of horrific dreams.

Moments later, my mom entered my bedroom with a garment bag.

I rubbed my face and fanned myself, still feeling overheated from the dream. "What's that?"

"Your dress for tonight. It's almost five." Mom walked to the end of my bed and draped it across my blanket.

"I gotta wear a dress?" I frowned. While I didn't mind dresses, I wasn't particularly fond of them, either. Especially in wintry weather. This was Colorado in November—not exactly tropical. I preferred my jeans and baggy hoodies.

Mom gave me a tight smile. "Yes."

"Because?" I asked.

"Because your grandfather is very old-fashioned, and we are trying to ease him back into our lives. He believes dinner should be a formal affair, so to appease him, we are going to follow his rules . . . for now." She seemed just as annoyed by the idea as I did.

I huffed. "Whatever." I rolled off the bed and grabbed the dress. "Can I wear my tennis shoes?"

Mom shook her head, and I fought back a pout. I hated dress shoes. Like really hated them.

"Are you okay? You look a little haggard." She gazed at me with concern.

"I'm fine. I just had a bad dream." I didn't really want to discuss it. I shuffled into my bathroom and hung the dress on the towel rack. After unzipping the garment bag, I slid it down to land in a pile on the floor.

"Hmm." It wasn't the worst thing I'd ever seen. The simple, light pink dress had an elegance about it. It had a round collar, three-quarter sleeves, and a princess seamed bodice. I slipped the dress over my head. I'm a petite person at five feet two inches tall, but this dress fell just below the knee, as I suspected it should have—like it was custom made for me.

I yelled through the doorway, "Mom, I need you to zip me up!"

She stepped inside and took a moment to look at me. "Oh, honey. It's beautiful on you." She smiled, and I could tell by the look in her eyes that this wasn't one of those mom-goggle moments. She meant what she'd said.

I glanced at myself in the mirror. I'd never felt particularly pretty before. My raven black hair landed just below my shoulder blades, and while it wasn't curly, it wasn't perfectly straight, either. My pale skin often stood out, even when I spent time in the sun. It seemed as if I was immune to tanning. I'd learned not to wear eyeliner too. When I did, it framed my blue-gray eyes in a way that made them look ominous. I couldn't count the number of times I'd been asked if I was into gothic stuff. I always replied, "No, I just naturally look like death."

Pink had never been a color I'd considered trying, but if this dress were any indication of all pink clothing, I thought I might reconsider that. I kinda felt pretty, or at least, not quite so much like a freak. Given what I'd just learned about myself earlier in the day, feeling somewhat normal was a good thing. I'd take it.

Mom ran her fingers through my hair, then gathered it on top of my head in a messy bun. "What do you think? Should we put it up?"

I shook my head. "Not if I don't have to."

Her reflection winked at me in the mirror. "No, you absolutely don't have to. We'll just pull the sides back so they aren't in your face."

I nodded and enjoyed that moment with my mom. I couldn't remember the last time she'd styled my hair for me. Probably because I'd always thrown a fit when she'd tried. But tonight, everything felt off. I wasn't going to shun the comfort of my mother's care, in any form. I needed her to be my calming presence, even if I still felt annoyance with her. She was exactly that.

We drove through an area called Havenwood Heights. As we passed several large estates, Dad explained that the homes in this area had been here for several generations. The one we were heading to was among the biggest homes on the street.

As we approached, I took notice of multicolored stones that towered upward, supporting dark shingles. I could make out several chimneys, and I silently wondered why anyone would need that many fireplaces. One corner of the house had a large round room that reminded me of a turret like on the old castles they always showed in horror movies.

Dad stopped the car in front of an impressive set of stone steps. My eyes were immediately drawn to the two large statues that flanked the entryway. Dragons. My hopes that I could temporarily forget about all this shifter business were immediately dashed.

A tall, broad-shouldered man in a suit and tie greeted my father at the bottom of the stairs. They shook hands and exchanged a few words I couldn't hear, then Dad motioned for us to exit the car and follow him. Mom waited for me to shut my door, then she clasped my hand in hers as we followed Dad up the stairs. I could feel the tension pulsing through her muscles. She was uncomfortable, and that made me even more apprehensive.

The man in the suit sat behind the wheel of our car and drove it around the side of the house and out of sight. Dad gave Mom and me a wink and pushed open the large oak doors. We stepped into the grandest entryway I'd ever seen, not that I had a lot to compare it to.

Tall beige walls connected to exquisitely polished oak flooring. An enormous crystal chandelier hung from the vaulted ceiling, projecting colorful sparkles on everything in the room. I struggled to tear my eyes away from its beauty. Dad stepped beside me and cleared his throat, so I moved my gaze from the crystal drops above to the elderly man who seemed to suddenly materialize in front of me.

"Lawrence Mills, I'd like to introduce you to your granddaughter, Zoey." He turned to me. "Zoey, this is your Grandpa Mills."

Grandpa stood about average height. His frame appeared wiry, and he had wild white hair that looked as if it took real effort to tame. His black suit was impeccable, and even his shoes were shined to perfection. He squinted his pale green eyes and leaned in a little closer. While his vision might have been somewhat impaired, I believed he was a shrewd man that didn't miss anything.

"She's a little wisp of a thing, isn't she." He stated that as a fact, not a question.

Dad placed a hand on my shoulder. "Yes, but she's mighty in spirit."

Grandpa's lips turned up a little at that. "I've no doubt she is. She's

17

a Mills!" Then he glanced at my mother. "Well, half Mills anyway." His voice held a hint of disgust.

Mom squeezed my hand a little tighter, but didn't reply. It signaled to me that I shouldn't worry about the insult. It would all be fine.

Dad put his arm around Mom. "Lawrence, if this is any indication of how the night will go, then I suggest we say our goodbyes now."

"Eh! Don't get your shorts in a wad, boy. Come on in and eat some dinner." He turned to go, taking his first step with a cane that looked every bit as old as he was. Before his second step, he turned his head toward my dad. "And stop calling me Lawrence. You know I hate that. I'm your father."

Dad shrugged. "No, I can't say that I do know what you hate. I don't remember much, thanks to this town's special wards."

I looked up at my mom.

"There's a spell on the town that makes people forget about Havenwood Falls and everyone in it. It becomes more like a vague dream." Mom glanced at Grandpa Mills. "Some people get their memories back in a rush, others in small chunks. Some memories trickle back in slowly. Dad and I are getting them back in little segments."

We followed Grandpa through a set of double doors and into a large, elegantly furnished dining room. The gleaming mahogany table looked as if it could have seated at least ten people. I tried not to openly gawk.

"Well, look who the cat dragged in," said a female voice from the back of the room.

Dad stood still for just a moment, then turned to the woman and smiled. "Jetta? Is that you?"

She gave an over-pronounced bow and then walked toward us. "In the flesh . . . for the moment." She smiled slyly as she seemed to take a moment to appreciate her own joke. Her skin-tight black dress looked as if it were made of leather, and matched her knee-high boots perfectly. Jetta's pixie-cut hair was a radiant silver color, and I thrilled to see her eyes were very similar to mine—a pale gray with blue mixed in. Despite the hair color, she appeared to be in her early twenties, with a vibrant energy about her.

Dad turned to address us then. "Bianca. Zoey. This is my younger sister, Jetta."

Aunt Jetta smiled. "It's wonderful to meet you, Zoey! And I remember Bianca, although I'm sure she doesn't remember me. Not yet, anyway." She gave my dad a small shove on his shoulder. "You stayed away far too long, big brother."

Dad shrugged. "If it hadn't been for Lawre . . . uh, Dad's letter, I wouldn't be here now."

Grandpa grunted out something I didn't understand, then barked an order. "Everyone sit down. I can't think or talk on an empty stomach."

We all took a seat at the table, and a kind-looking older woman entered the dining room with a wheeled tray full of all kinds of meats and vegetables. She made her way around the table, filling plates while no one said a word. The tension was too much for me, and I couldn't resist the urge to say something to break the silence. I looked over at Aunt Jetta and took in her appearance. Several beautiful pieces of jewelry graced her neck, arms, and fingers. She also had quite a few tattoos, and I found that fascinating.

"I like your piercings, Aunt Jetta." I tried to make it sound as cheerful as possible.

Aunt Jetta reached up and ran a finger over the gold hoop in her eyebrow, then the diamond stud in her nose. She had several in her ears too, but they weren't as unusual. "Thanks, kiddo. I'm glad someone in this family appreciates individuality." She shot a frustrated look at Grandpa.

Grandpa snorted. "You look like a damn pin cushion."

Jetta batted her eyelashes at him dramatically. "Aw, I love you too, Daddy."

Grandpa just snorted again and picked at his food.

*Well, I guess asking about her tattoos is a bad idea. I'll save that for another time.*

Dad spoke up next. "So, Dad, tell me why we're here."

Grandpa looked at him like he'd sprouted a second head. "To eat, you moron."

"No, I mean why did you really summon my family to

Havenwood Falls? My memories are still a bit fuzzy, but I do clearly remember you telling Bianca and me you never wanted to see us again."

My eyes grew wide. *Harsh!* Dad started right off with the elephant in the room. He didn't just mention it—he shot it between the eyes.

I noticed Mom fidget a little in her seat. I reached over and took her hand in mine. I felt her relax a little.

Grandpa stared Dad down a moment, then placed his fork beside his plate. One bushy white eyebrow rose as he spoke. "To be frank, I'm getting old. We dragons aren't immortal, and someone needs to carry on the Mills legacy. It's gotta be you."

Aunt Jetta laughed out loud. "Yes, darling brother, it has to be you. Do you want to know why?" She glanced at Grandpa, then back at my dad. "Because the old man here still won't forgive me for wanting to be my own person."

Dad looked at them both. "When are you gonna bury that hatchet? It's been years!"

Grandpa shook his head. "I can't abide defiance and disobedience."

It was Dad's turn to laugh. "But you're forgiving mine?"

The room became so quiet, you could've heard a pin drop.

"No," said Dad. "You aren't. You just wanted me back here so I can be under your thumb. If you still can't accept Bianca as a part of this family, then we have nothing more to talk about." He stood. "Girls, it's time we left."

Grandpa stood as well. "Now, wait a minute. You can't just come in here—"

Dad cut him off. "When you're ready to act like a proper father and grandfather, you know where to find us. Until then, don't bother."

Grandpa roared, and it shook the windows. It wasn't merely a loud yell. It was the kind of supernatural sound that made the very ground quake beneath your feet. I clung to my mom as I watched Grandpa's eyes change from pale to a vivid green with a narrow slit for a pupil.

Aunt Jetta put a hand on Grandpa's shoulder. "Dad, calm down. Keep that up, and you'll have the Court here."

Grandpa closed his eyes, then sat back down in his chair. He took a deep breath. "Does she have it, Tristan?" he asked quietly.

Dad looked at me, then back at Grandpa. "Yes, she has the gene."

"May I talk to her?" He sounded exhausted.

Dad studied Grandpa for a moment, then turned to me. "Your grandpa would like a word with you. Are you comfortable with that? If not, you can say no."

I looked at my grandfather. He seemed to have calmed down now. "Sure, I don't mind." I wasn't quite as brave as I tried to sound, but this man was family, and I knew Dad wouldn't allow him to hurt me.

Aunt Jetta walked to where we stood and put her arm around my mom. "Let's get reacquainted while they chat." Mom looked at me, and I nodded my head.

"I'll be fine, Mom. Go ahead." I pasted on a smile to reassure her.

"Okay, if you're sure." Mom looked at Grandpa. "I don't care how you feel about me, but don't you dare disrespect my daughter." She shot him a fierce and protective glare I'd never seen her give anyone.

Grandpa sent her a silent nod, and Aunt Jetta led her out of the dining room.

Dad put a hand on my shoulder. "I'll be just outside these doors if you need me."

I gave him a thumbs up, and he winked at me, then shut the doors behind him.

There I stood—alone in a huge room with a cranky grandfather I'd just met, who happened to be a dragon. What could possibly go wrong?

I took the seat next to Grandpa and tried to calm my nerves. He was intimidating.

"You probably don't know a lot about our family history yet. Would you like me to fill you in?"

I nodded my head. "That'd be nice. Thank you."

He leaned back and closed his eyes a moment before focusing his gaze back on me. "Settle in, Zoey. It's a long story."

# CHAPTER 3

"Family records go back far enough to indicate that Iceland is where we originated. My father, his father, and his father's father were all frost dragon shifters. Obviously, we didn't start out that way. In the beginning, we were fierce, mostly solitary beings —protective of the resources in our lands. Dragon families would grow together, then scatter to make our own homes and families. When humans began to settle in our area, it was a source of constant conflict." Grandpa Mills frowned as he relayed our history. "No matter the intention, it always ended in a bloody battle. Both sides became exhausted and broken, tired of losing members. After one particularly devastating loss for the humans, a sorcerer approached us with a proposition. Due to his magic, he could speak to us much the way we communicate with each other. He said that if we'd allow him to change us into humans on occasion, we could communicate with their king and work on a peace treaty."

I felt my eyes grow wide. "Seriously?"

He nodded. "It's the truth. So, we talked among ourselves, and a few volunteered for the task."

He grew quiet and pensive.

When it seemed he wouldn't continue, I had to ask him, "What happened next?"

His eyes snapped to mine. "The humans betrayed our trust. The sorcerer worked for the king, and our agreeing to the deal was all that it took to change our entire clan into humans. They changed us, then attacked us. As humans, we were as vulnerable as they, or so they believed." His lips turned up into a wicked grin. "But there was a kink in their plan. When threatened, our dragons emerged to protect us. We wiped out the entire kingdom after that."

My jaw dropped. "You killed them all?"

"I didn't. I wasn't around. Our ancestors did." He shrugged. "This is the story that's been passed down for generations. I don't know if it's one hundred percent accurate, but it's close enough."

He sighed. "The humans kept coming, and eventually, we had to learn to hide among them to survive without casualties. When we heard news of a journey to this continent, and the search for sanctuary, our family decided to tag along."

It was a lot to take in. "Is there anything else I should know?" Fear almost kept me from asking.

"I think you know the most important parts. There are trivial things. We tend to be paler than most humans and can't tan no matter how hard we try. The details are unclear to me. Evolution to adapt to our climate or some kind of genetic hokum." He waved his hand around as if it was of no consequence, then tapped his index finger on his bottom lip as he reflected on his next words. "I hear you like jewelry."

I nodded, wondering about the sudden change of topic. "I do."

"You've heard the tales of dragons and treasure?"

I nodded again.

"All legends start from a truth. Our truth is that we have an affinity for beautiful things. Jewelry certainly falls into that category. It's in your blood, so to speak."

I felt a sense of relief at his words. At least I had a reason for my obsession, outside of just being odd.

"Other things you'll likely notice," he said, "you may prefer solitude to large crowds. What do they call that now?" He took a moment to think. "Introverts. Yes, that's it. Dragons are generally solitary creatures, although with frost dragons, we do sometimes exist

AMY HALE

in small clans, such as our ancestors did. The human side of us craves family and companionship, which is why we now do our best to exist in peace with each other, as well as other creatures." He scowled, as if the thought of coexistence angered him.

"You don't like this arrangement?" I asked.

He turned his gaze to mine, and his eyes felt like they were boring into my soul. I adjusted myself in the chair, trying to shake the discomfort of his stare.

"I tolerate it," he stated. "Humans are the reason we are in this mess, so I have very little use for them. But we do what we must, and I am willing to grant concessions . . . for now."

The way he said "for now" sent a chill down my spine. I amended my earlier thought. At that moment, he wasn't intimidating—he was terrifying.

Grandpa Mills crossed his legs and then pointed to my hand, noticing the bandage. "What happened there?"

"I had an accident. A burn." I glanced down at my hand.

"How is it now?" His words indicated a question, but his expression spoke volumes. He knew what my answer would be.

"It's healing . . . under the scale." I pulled the bandage off and pushed my hand forward to allow him a look.

He nodded. "One of the numerous benefits of being a frost dragon. When needed, we can create frost, ice, and blasts of arctic air at will."

I pondered that for a moment.

"What other uses does it have, besides the obvious?" I asked as I held up my hand.

"Well, you can cool a drink in no time flat." He winked at me, and I was taken aback by the levity of his demeanor. He'd been so grouchy just moments before.

"There was a time when we froze our food, for consumption later. It's not so necessary with modern technology, but when I was young, it was all we had."

"When exactly was that, if you don't mind my asking?" I couldn't help but be intensely curious as to his real age. He looked to be in his eighties, but I felt sure he was much older.

24

"I'm almost two hundred, give or take a few years." He scratched his chin absentmindedly. "I was in my early twenties when we relocated from the old country. My family joined the original band of travelers searching for sanctuary. In 1854, they discovered what we now know as Havenwood Falls."

My mouth gaped open. "Two hundred? That's insane!" I couldn't decide if that could be classified as awesome or horrifying. "How long do frost dragons live?"

His expression grew sad. "Not long enough. Once we hit twenty, we age about half the rate of humans. I'm nearing the end of my lifespan."

I could feel a bit of sadness creep over me. I didn't know this man at all, and he didn't appear to be a popular member of the family, yet the thought of losing him hit me deeply. It made no sense.

"It's okay, child. When I go, I'll be with your Grandma Christine again. I can't ask for anything better." He patted my hand, and for a moment, I felt a kindness he withheld from the rest of the world.

"How long has she been gone?" I asked with a quiet reverence.

"I lost her in the Massacre of 1876." He paused and his expression grew hard. "I lost of lot of family and friends that day."

"Massacre?" I felt the word stick in my throat.

His eyebrows drew together, almost meeting in the middle. "You'll learn about it at school." He stood abruptly and gripped his cane so tightly, I thought I heard it crack.

"I will?" I wasn't quite sure what that meant.

"What are you, a parrot? Yes, you'll get the public version. The real events of that day are only known to a few of the humans that live here. It's not something we discuss openly." He began to hobble toward the door.

I sat motionless, trying to grasp all the information I'd gleaned so far.

He turned and glared at me, his intimidating side returning full force. "Well, girl, are you gonna sit there all night? Let's get your parents back in here so we can eat before the meal is completely ruined."

I returned to the seat I'd occupied before everyone left. My appetite had abandoned me.

~

TWO WEEKS HAD PASSED since I'd learned the truth about my family. I'd had a lot of time to think about my true identity. I'd once believed there was nothing special about me. The last two schools I had attended had hammered that point home. A month ago, I existed as just a below-average teen girl, approaching her sweet sixteen and wishing she could be someone else. Anyone else.

Don't get me wrong. I loved my parents, and I really had nothing to complain about, but I didn't like me. Despite all the "you must love yourself first" stuff my parents had fed me every time I'd been snubbed or my heart had been broken, I knew the truth. I was a weirdo, and I always had been. But the joke was on me. Weird didn't begin to cover it. What was sad was that I now lived in a town full of weirdos, and I still didn't feel like I fit in.

My mom used to call me unique and say that's why I didn't click with people easily. She said, and I quote, "Average people don't understand you, so they lose out on an amazing friendship. Only people that are very special will bond with someone as amazing as you."

The previous times she'd said that, I'd think "Yeah. I wish." But knowing what I knew now, a lot of things made sense. I was beginning to understand the logic behind our love for this part of the United States. We were evolved for a snowy climate—one of many reasons Havenwood Falls was a perfect home for us. The closer my birthday loomed, the more I found the cold comforting. While my schoolmates wore heavy coats, I fought the urge to wear T-shirts.

There was also my tendency to be introverted. I'd generally rather read than attend parties. That part, coupled with my unusual looks, had caused me a butt-load of grief growing up.

The day after I learned the truth, Dad took Mom and me to meet the Court of the Sun and the Moon. As a supernatural being, I had to be registered, per the Court's law. I also had to get a tattoo. Sounds cool for a soon-to-be sixteen-year-old, but the bummer part was nobody could see it. Magic tattoos, secret councils, and a town full of all the scary things the human world was told didn't exist. Once I adjusted to the idea, I realized it was kinda cool. Too bad I had to keep this secret hidden. I felt like the one thing that made me interesting, I couldn't tell anyone. The existence of non-human beings had to be kept secret. This rule kept us safe. It was the reason Havenwood Falls existed.

I pondered all of this new information and exhaled a deep sigh as I watched the scenery fly by the passenger-side window of my dad's car. It was the end of November, and I'd been incident-free since the coffee shop accident, so I naively wished that'd be all there was to it. To be honest, the idea of becoming a full-blown dragon terrified me, especially since I didn't know how the transformation process worked. No one had given me answers for that, and I'd been afraid to ask. I wanted to know, but I also didn't. Sometimes knowing can make the anxiety worse, like getting a shot. If you find out at the last minute, you won't waste time worrying about it before hand. Only, I still worried. I was making myself crazy with all the back and forth of emotions and thoughts, and my birthday approached quickly.

I released another big sigh, overwhelmed by it all, and I felt Dad shift in his seat. I wasn't intentionally trying to make him feel bad. But with every little noise or gesture, he seemed more and more displeased. Guilt sucked. It wasn't his fault that I'd never been the kind of girl to make friends easily. The new school was nice, but he knew I struggled to find my place, as usual.

We pulled up in front of the school, and Dad forced a smile. "I know it's been rough, kiddo. I'm sorry. We never meant to put you through all of . . ." He paused and gestured around him. ". . . this."

I shrugged. "I'll survive." I reached over and gave his arm a squeeze. "It'll just take some time for me to adjust to . . ." I mimicked his gesture. ". . . this."

He chuckled. "All right, sweetheart. You'd better get to class. I'll talk to you tonight."

I nodded and stepped out of the car. I shut the door and glanced up at the large brick building in front of me. My teachers were nice enough, and there were a few students that I kind of liked. The only person that had really made an effort to befriend me was Miranda Saunders, a very kind girl with platinum blond hair, porcelain skin, and a perfect, heart-shaped face. She stood a good four inches taller than me as well. She was the kind of girl that it would be easy to be jealous of, if she weren't so sweet.

I pushed through the doors and saw her standing next to my locker. As usual, she was dressed impeccably in designer jeans, a gorgeous blue sweater, and uncomfortable-looking wedge shoes that added unneeded inches to her height. She looked like she had just stepped off the pages of a fashion magazine.

"Oh, hey, Zoey!" Her wide smile greeted me. "Did you study for that English quiz Mr. Zander is giving us today?"

I tried not to laugh. "I did. How about you?"

I pulled books out of my locker while pretending not to watch her reaction.

"Of course, although if I don't do well, I may have to ask for tutoring." She grinned.

I couldn't hold back my laugh this time. "I knew it! You are totally trying to find a reason to stay after class."

Her expression changed to one of horror, as if I'd insulted her. "Me? Whatever makes you think that?"

I turned to face her. "How about because all you ever do is talk about how hot Mr. Zander is and how you wish he were younger, or you were older?"

Miranda batted her long lashes at me. "I will admit to no such thing." She smirked and sighed. "But I will admit he's fun to look at."

I shook my head. "True, but it's still disturbing."

She gave me a wink and then turned her head in the direction of our classroom. "We should get going."

I picked up my English book and followed her. I'd only glanced down a moment when I ran into something warm and solid.

I raised my head to see a Havenwood Falls T-shirt at eye level. It covered what felt like an impressively muscled chest. I felt myself blush at my blunder and looked up into the exquisite face of one Jordan Woods.

Jordan was an Adonis in blue jeans. His shaggy blond hair, bright blue eyes, and chiseled jawline pulled me in every time I set eyes on him. I felt my nerves kick up a notch.

"Oh, gosh. I'm so sorry. I should have been watching where I walked." I hoped I wasn't mumbling, since I tended to do that when I got nervous. I could almost hear the blood rushing to my face as I blushed.

"No problem." He looked me over for a moment. "Aren't you the new girl? Zoey? Your dad runs the pawn shop now, right?"

I nodded, suddenly losing my ability to speak. I'd never actually spoken to Jordan face to face before this, but I'd silently worshiped him from afar.

"Cool. Well, I guess I'll see you around. Have a nice day." He smiled at me and continued to his first-period class.

It took a moment for me to breathe. That smile almost melted my knees. When I took my next step, my legs shook a bit, and suddenly Miranda stood right next to me. "He's cute, huh? You should totally flirt with him."

"Me?" I squeaked. "I struggled to complete a sentence just now. Flirting will be impossible."

"Don't let him fluster you. He's only human, like the rest of us." She smiled, but it didn't reach her eyes.

"Sure, like the rest of us." I didn't say more. Instead I walked to class and pondered the fact that I didn't know who was human and who wasn't. *Shouldn't I sense something? Would this be one of those things that develops after my birthday?* I really hoped all this started making sense soon. I felt as if I were losing my mind, and I was sure an insane dragon wandering Havenwood Falls was the last thing anyone needed.

THE CLOCK slowly ticked away as I watched from my desk in the back of the room. Lunch was minutes away, and I was more than ready. I'd overslept and skipped breakfast, so I paid the price. It felt like my stomach was devouring itself, and if I didn't eat soon, it would growl so loud that everyone in class would hear it. Thankfully, most of the other students were engrossed in their history books and showed no indication that they'd heard the smaller rumblings coming from my stomach. I tried to focus, but I just couldn't get into the Civil War at that moment. My preoccupied mind struggled with everything else, and I couldn't concentrate. I had so many questions.

*How many of the kids around me are supernatural, too? What if I do something wrong and get in trouble with the Court? Am I in danger from any of the other supernatural beings that live here? Is my mom safe, since she's human?*

The bell rang, and I slowly gathered my books. I still ran these questions through my mind when Miranda hooked her arm through mine.

"Ready for lunch?" She sounded chipper as always.

"Yes, so ready. I'm starving." I groaned.

Arm in arm, we walked to the cafeteria. She placed her lunch box on the table, and I frowned.

"Do you have something against cafeteria food? You always bring your lunch." I teased her, although I did wonder if there was something about our school lunches that she wasn't telling me.

"No, not at all. It's just that I'm on a special diet. Food allergies and all that."

"Oh, okay. You'll have to let me know what they are so I don't accidentally give you something you can't have." The thought of making my best friend, really my only friend, sick, worried me. I'd never forgive myself if I accidentally hurt her.

She smiled and waved me away. "It's all good. Now go get your lunch and get back so we can chat."

I stuck my hands in the pockets of my jeans and strolled over to the lunch line. It moved quickly, and I arrived at the food trays in no time. I watched the line worker place pizza in the middle of the plate, then set a fruit cup and salad on the sides. She raised her eyes to mine and asked, "Milk?"

I shook my head no. "Water will be fine."

She nodded and handed me a bottle of water along with my food tray.

I'd almost made it back to my seat when I noticed Miranda

appeared as if she were about to be sick all over the table. I rushed over to her, setting my tray aside so it wasn't in my way.

"Are you okay? You don't look well." I put my hand in hers, and it felt unusually cold.

"Yeah, I just think my lunch isn't agreeing with me." She raised a hand to her mouth and covered it.

I grabbed the thermos she'd been sipping from to inspect the contents. Miranda reached for it, but wasn't fast enough to get to it before I did. I sloshed the contents around inside.

"What is this, soup? Is this one of your food allergies?" I tilted the insulated thermos to get a better look.

"Uh, yeah. My lunch must have gotten tainted." She reached for the thermos again, and I handed it to her, spilling a little on the table. I grabbed a napkin to wipe it up and then froze.

"Miranda, is that what I think it is?" My eyes grew wide as I looked into hers.

She put the lid on her thermos, stood, and grabbed her things. "I gotta go."

I stood, too, forgetting all about my pizza and salad. Shoot, I don't think I could have eaten anyway. Not after what I just saw.

I gave the table a quick swipe with the napkin before I followed her out of the cafeteria, down the hall, and into the girls' bathroom. She ducked into a stall and quickly slammed the door.

"Miranda, you can talk to me. I promise to be open-minded," I said quietly.

"I don't think so," she said, just before I heard her start to puke.

I waited patiently until she had purged it all from her system. She flushed and opened the door, then jumped when she realized I was still there.

"You didn't have to wait," she muttered.

"I know, but I wanted to." I smiled at her.

Miranda turned on the water and washed her hands.

I moved to stand beside her. "I can keep a secret. I'm getting good at that, actually. I may even have a big secret of my own." I gave her a wink, hoping it would encourage her.

"You do?" Her voice sounded hopeful.

"I do." I placed a hand on her arm. "So, let's make a deal. You tell me yours, and I'll tell you mine?"

She nodded. "Okay." She took a deep breath. "My lunch is probably what you thought it was. Except that it wasn't my usual. Mom must have accidentally put her lunch in my thermos by mistake."

"You don't drink the same . . . uh . . . stuff?" I didn't know if I could get the word blood past my lips just yet. I ducked my head down to be sure no one else occupied the stalls behind us. I knew it wouldn't do to have someone overhear our conversation.

Miranda dried her hands. "No, I'm very particular about my meals. They must be from animal sources. I don't like the taste of . . . well, the usual sources."

I raised my eyebrows. "So, you're like the vegan version of your kind?"

She chuckled. "Yeah, something like that."

"That's pretty cool," I said. I still thought it was gross, but it didn't surprise me that drinking human blood would upset her. Her kind nature wouldn't allow for anything else.

She smiled at me. "Thank you. I'm glad we're friends, Zoey." She pulled me in for a hug.

I hugged her back. "Me, too, Miranda."

*Holy crap. My best friend is a vampire.*

# CHAPTER 4

*M*iranda leaned against the sink and crossed her arms. "My mom and I are both vampires. I'm kind of a freak, in more ways than one. My mom had a short relationship with the man that fathered me. Once she found out she was pregnant, he bolted, so I've never met him. What makes all this unique is he's a vampire and changed my mom before I was born . . . before they found out about the pregnancy. As a rule, vampires aren't supposed to be able to sire children, at least that's what I've heard, so he became irate, accusing her of cheating on him. She'd been changed, but I was born this way. I'm not the norm."

She sighed. "I'm also kind of an outcast because I prefer animals over the blood bank stuff." She frowned. "The others of my kind do their best to avoid me." Her voice held a hint of sadness and I couldn't help but place my hand over hers.

"They don't know what a great person they're missing out on." Great, I'm turning into my mother.

She squinted her eyes at me in suspicion, but I sensed a teasing tone to her voice. "Get that line from your mom?"

I laughed. "Was it an obvious mom-ism?"

She nodded. "It was. And I've heard it a million times from my own mother."

We both stood in silence for a moment, then I spoke up. "Maybe they actually know what they're talking about now and then."

Miranda nodded again. "Well, the plus side is I'm pretty popular with the humans in the school. It's mostly just the vamps that have labeled me a pariah."

I let out a huff. "Yeah, well count yourself lucky. I can't seem to get anyone, humans or otherwise, to give me the time of day, unless they are picking on me." I paused and looked at my best friend. "Why are you so nice to me?"

She reached out and put a hand on my shoulder. "How could I not be? You exude kindness and compassion, Zoey. I knew the moment I saw you that you were special."

That made me smile, and blush a little. "Thank you. I think that's the kindest thing anyone has ever said to me."

"You deserve kindness."

I didn't know how to respond to that, so I changed the subject. "You've haven't heard my secret yet. It's only fair."

Miranda's eyes lit up. "Yes! Tell me!"

I took a deep breath. This would have been the first time I admitted my secret to anyone, but since Miranda had a secret of her own, I felt safe with her. I still worked to push the words past my lips. "I'm not human, either."

She shrugged. "I figured as much. I know you aren't a vampire, so . . ." She waited for me to fill in the blanks.

"I'm a frost dragon." I tried to mask the insecurity in my voice.

"A dragon!" she squealed.

"Shhh!" I hissed. "Not so loud."

"Sorry." She bounced up and down. "But that's just the coolest thing I've ever heard."

"With all the supes that live in this town, that's the coolest thing?"

She chuckled. "I've always been fascinated with dragons, so I might be a little biased. A frost dragon? So, you breathe ice instead of fire?"

I nodded. "Something like that."

"Awesome," she whispered beneath her breath. Miranda's eyes widened. "Oh my God, Zoey! You have to meet Bale! He's a dragon shifter, too! He's not a frost dragon, but still . . . you guys would probably have a lot in common."

I shook my head. "Not yet, Miranda. I recently found out myself, and I'm doing all I can to hold it together right now. Maybe after the dust has settled."

Miranda nodded. "I get it. There's a lot to adjust to."

She placed her hand on my arm in a gesture of support. It was good to know, though, that there were others kinda like me. And to have a friend like Miranda.

~

THE REST of the day went by quickly. Since I'd skipped lunch, I managed to keep my hunger at bay by quickly choking down some pretzels I'd bought from a vending machine between fifth and sixth periods. Miranda felt much better and even a little giddy after I'd told her my secret. She thought being a dragon was great, although I couldn't verify or deny that for her either way, since I hadn't actually experienced it yet.

We were walking to our last class of the day, when a girl I didn't recognize shoved me into a wall and knocked the books from my hands.

"What hole did you crawl out of, freak?" She growled the words at me.

I glanced up into her face and saw a lot of anger and hatred. It was nothing unusual for me—this was just a repeat of my past school experiences.

Miranda's voice came from my left. "Leave her alone, Katy. She isn't bothering anyone."

Katy turned her glare on Miranda. Her dark, short-bobbed hair swung as she stepped closer. "Who's gonna make me? You?"

Miranda closed her eyes, and Katy smiled. Katy must have thought she frightened Miranda, but in reality, I believed Miranda worked to control her temper. She gave off a vibe that reeked of danger.

I placed a hand on Miranda's arm. "It's okay. I'm not hurt." I turned to Katy. "I'm Zoey Mills. It's nice to meet you." *Kill them with kindness, right?*

"I know who you are. I've heard all about your family. You aren't welcome here." She put a finger in my face. "If you knew what was good for you, you'd move away—all of you." With that, she stomped away. I watched her retreat and tried to understand what my family had to do with anything.

I turned my face to Miranda's and whispered, "Is it possible she knows? Is she supernatural, too?"

Miranda shook her head. "She's human, but her dad is one of the few in town that know of our existence. He's not supposed to speak of it, so I'm wondering if she overheard something she shouldn't have."

"About my family?" I squeaked.

"Well," said Miranda, "you are the newcomers in town. A little place like this . . . there will be talk. Granted, it's usually in the form of your usual gossip, not about what species someone is."

I nodded. "Well, whatever she heard, she must not have liked it. I'm not a stranger to bullying or people thinking I'm odd, but it would have been nice to go a bit longer before it started up."

Miranda's smile held sadness. "We won't allow her to push you around, Zoey. I promise."

I nodded, thankful for someone willing to stand by me. I pulled her in for a hug and wiped a tear from my eye. "I don't know why I'm so emotional. I thought this kind of thing wouldn't bother me anymore."

She squeezed me and bent down to help me gather my books. "Let's get to class and get this day over with."

THE FOLLOWING DAY, the school buzzed with talk of something called the Cold Moon Ball. It was a large celebration that took place every year during the Cold Moon. That seemed cool, especially since this year the Cold Moon and my birthday landed on the same day: December third. I took a flier from a stack sitting near the entryway of the school and scanned the information. I was shocked to learn that the dance itself was a ball held in my grandfather's house, a charity event people flocked to. To be honest, I didn't see my grandfather as the charitable type. But it appeared to be something everyone looked forward to, if the excitement surrounding the announcement was anything to gauge by, so I guess his grumpiness didn't scare off everyone in town.

A shout caught my attention, and I turned to find a freshman named Marty glaring at an older student named Gary. Marty had been hanging chess club posters on the main bulletin board, and it seemed that Gary had been hassling him.

Gary shoved Marty, so Marty shoved back.

In one swift move, Gary put Marty in a headlock. "Stay out of my way next time, you little jerk."

Marty struggled. "Let me go!"

Everyone witnessed the aggressive behavior, but did nothing.

Jordan Woods jogged past me as I watched in dismay. "Gary, leave him alone. Don't you have better things to do, man?"

Gary sent Jordan an angry scowl. "Mind your own business, meathead. Marty and I are just having a little fun."

Jordan stepped forward and grabbed Gary's arm. "Let. Him. Go."

He now stood nose to nose with the bully.

Gary released Marty, and the freshman hit the floor as he began to gasp for air.

"Maybe I should let you take his place," Gary snarled.

I moved closer, wondering if I could somehow help, but also knowing that being the new girl in school, my help may not be appreciated.

Jordan crossed his arms. "If you think you're big enough, then go for it."

Gary stared at him for a long moment, then spit his gum on the floor in front of Jordan. "You're a waste of my time."

He turned to leave.

"Keep in mind that Marty, and any other student at this school, will also be a waste of your time. If you bother them, you bother me."

Gary adjusted his jacket and pretended not to care about Jordan's threat. "Whatever." He gave Marty one last glare before strolling down the hall, away from the snickering students.

As someone who'd been bullied most of my life, I appreciated what Jordan had done. Marty had Jordan on his side, and Gary wasn't likely to pester him again. I was going to step up and help pick up the posters Marty had been hanging, but Jordan beat me to it. He gathered the posters and helped Marty to his feet.

"You okay, buddy?" Jordan asked, dropping a hand on Marty's shoulder.

"Yeah, I'm good," Marty mumbled, embarrassment coloring his cheeks.

Jordan handed all but one flyer to Marty. "Chess club, huh?"

Marty nodded silently.

"I've never learned to play chess. If I join, will they teach me?"

Marty nodded once more.

"Is it hard?" asked Jordan.

"Not once you learn the pieces." Marty's fingers flipped the edge of his poster stack nervously.

"Can you teach me? I'd love to at least know the basics before I start playing against anyone." Jordan's expression was sincere.

Marty's eyes lit up. "Sure! I'm free just about any time after school."

"Awesome." Jordan clapped Marty on the back. "I'm looking forward to hanging out with you." He folded the flyer and put it in his back pocket. "See you after last period."

Marty walked away with his head held high and a smile on his face. True joy formed his expression.

My heart thumped wildly in my chest. I'd already thought Jordan was cute, but this made him angelic. He came across like a knight in shining armor. Except in this weird scenario, I was the dragon he'd normally expect to slay, not fall in love with. I groaned at the thought of him finding out my secret. I turned and stuffed the Cold Moon Ball flier inside one of my notebooks.

"Hi." A familiar voice spoke softly near my ear.

I looked up to see Jordan smiling at me.

"You gonna go to the ball this year?" he asked.

"I . . . I don't know. I'm just now learning about it." I tried not to let the butterflies in my stomach make my voice shake.

"It's pretty fun. We go every year." He chuckled. "I'm surprised you don't already have the inside scoop, seeing as your grandpa runs it."

I smiled. "Yeah, you'd think I'd know all about it already."

"You should definitely go." He continued to smile at me.

"Okay, maybe I will." *Am I flirting? Oh God. I'm actually flirting.*

His grin widened. "Maybe you should go with me. I mean, I'm an old pro at this. My mom has been taking me since first grade. I can show you around the event and help you learn the history behind it, if your grandpa hasn't already explained it to you."

I bit my bottom lip. "Yeah, that might be fun."

He looked down at his shoes, then back up at me. I thought I detected a slight blush. Adorable. "Great, it's a date then." His smile was wide. I nodded, and he waved as he began to walk away. "Talk to you later, Zoey."

"Sure," I mumbled.

Within seconds, Miranda appeared at my side. "Oh my God! You are going to the ball with Jordan? That's so awesome!"

My mouth fell open. "How did you know? He just asked me. And how are you always next to me so quickly?"

She smirked and looked around, then leaned in. "Vampire. We're fast and have great hearing. It's awesome, until you hear a fight. Or your parents doing it in the next room."

"Ew!" I laughed.

"I know. Some things you can never un-hear." She shuddered.

I smiled again. "Have I told you how much I adore you, Miranda? 'Cause I do."

She flipped her blond hair off her shoulder and stuck her nose in the air regally. "Of course you do, daahling. Everyone adores me." We both burst out in laughter.

~

I RODE through the rest of the day on a cloud of happiness. Not only did I have an amazing best friend, but I had a date. With the cutest boy in school, no less. A small part of my mind wondered if it was some kind of cruel prank, but I couldn't let fear or negativity cloud my ability to at least attempt to have fun.

I said goodbye to Miranda on the front steps of the school as her mom pulled up to the curb. My dad had texted me to say he was running late, so I decided to hang out on one of the benches at Cook's Corner Park across the street—a nice quiet little spot under a tree that provided a magnificent view of the block but still gave the feeling of privacy. The park itself was beautiful, with vine-covered arches, stone paths, and a bronze fountain as the centerpiece. I couldn't wait to see what it was like in the spring. The spot I'd chosen allowed me to leave the snowball fights and noisy students behind, and I could imagine settling down in this spot with a good book when I had some free time.

I sat with my back to the large elm tree and pulled my phone from my pocket. The signal was really spotty at the moment, but I could kill time with a solitaire game. I'd just made my first play when I heard voices from behind me.

"Oh look, it's Zoey the emo girl," snarled Katy.

I frowned. *Not now. Not when everything else today had been so nice.* I turned around on the seat and saw Katy and two of her friends standing there.

I didn't like confrontation, so I tried to think of ways to keep this encounter from going south. "Hi. Am I in your spot? I can move if you'd like me to." I tried to form a friendly smile.

"Oh, I'd like you to move all right. All the way back to where you came from in Freakland." Her smile was cruel and sinister.

I stood to walk away, and one of her friends ran around me to block my path. "Where do you think you're going?"

I looked up at her. She was several inches taller than me and quite a bit larger overall. If I had to guess, I'd say all three of these girls were athletes.

"Listen, I don't want any trouble." I tried to sound polite.

Katy stepped next to her friend, further blocking my path. "Then maybe you shouldn't be flirting with Jordan Woods."

"Jordan?" I asked. "I barely know him. I've only talked to him a couple of times."

"But you're going to the Cold Moon Ball with him," Katy said.

"Well, he did ask me today, and I said yes." I paused. "Is he your boyfriend? If so, I swear I didn't know."

"No," scoffed Katy. "He's not my boyfriend, but don't get any ideas that he's yours, either. You don't belong here, and you don't belong with him."

I frowned. "Listen, I don't know what I did to make you upset with me, but if you'd—"

Katy interrupted me with a hard slap to the face. Stunned, I didn't know how to react. I'd been called names, screamed at, and teased mercilessly, but I'd never been physically assaulted before.

Katy laughed. "Did I smack some sense into you? Or do I need to do it again?"

Her friends laughed, and I took a moment to catch my breath. My face stung, and I worried her attack had left a mark. I closed my eyes, trying to control my emotions. My eyes began to burn as the tears filled my lashes. *I will not cry in front of her. I will not give her that satisfaction.*

I turned around to wipe my face, knowing that she and her goons were just as likely to strike with my back turned. I didn't care. I had an intense need to rein in my slowly building anger. Anger and heartbreak were emotions familiar to me, but this time something felt different. My hands began to shake, and when I opened my eyes, the world seemed slightly dimmer. I glanced down at my still trembling hands and saw my fingernails begin to grow into claws.

My hearing instantly amplified, and I could hear the three girls whisper behind me.

"What a crybaby. She should run home to mama," said one.

I heard another breathe out a shaky sigh.

Katy chuckled. "Let's give her something to really cry about."

The crunch of snow sounded the alarm that Katy was moving. I heard the sounds of something being picked up and then more crunching. My instincts kicked in, and I ducked just as a large pebble-filled snowball flew past me and hit the tree. I stood, ready to turn and defend myself, but terrified of what I might do. I started to panic. *Not here! Not now!* I knew my dragon was once again trying to protect me. I appreciated it, and to be honest, a part of me wanted to see these girls running away in fear, but I knew this was not the right answer. Not at this time. Not when I didn't yet know what I was capable of or how to control it.

Salvation stepped up in the form of my father. "What seems to be the trouble here, girls?"

I closed my eyes and forced my hands to relax, slowly feeling my claws retract.

Katy spoke for the group. "Nothing, just having a snowball fight."

I heard the other girls murmur in agreement.

"Ah, well, I think it's time we all moved on, don't you?" His calm voice had an edge to it that held anger as well.

The three girls said nothing as they walked away. Dad placed his hands on my shoulders. "Are you all right, sweetheart?"

I nodded, but couldn't yet find my voice.

"Are you sure?" He turned me to face him.

I looked up, letting the tears spill down my cheeks.

He gave me a small smile. "I see you've had a new experience with your dragon. I'm just sorry it happened at the hands of those horrible girls."

I nodded. "I'll be fine."

He pulled me to him and wrapped his arms around me protectively. "Yes, you will. You'll be better than fine."

I hoped and prayed he was right.

AT DINNER THAT NIGHT, Mom asked me about the incident with the girls.

"Do you really want me to rehash it?" I asked.

"I don't want to know about the girls. I want to know about you. What happened to you? Did your vision turn cloudy?" Concern laced her voice.

"It did for a little while." I picked up my spoon and tried to use it as a mirror. "Do my eyes look weird or something?" I gasped and dropped the spoon. "Did they change like Grandpa's did?"

Dad nodded. "A little, but they are normal now. My vision always becomes cloudy just before my eyes change. It happens quickly now, but in the beginning, it was a slower process."

At that moment, I was so glad I hadn't turned around during the assault. My eyes already seemed a little odd to people, with their mostly gray coloring. I could just imagine what Katy would have said or done if she'd seen dragon eyes instead of human.

"Once your vision clears, it becomes very sharp. You can see for miles, most of the time. Your hearing is also intensified." He smiled, giving me the impression he enjoyed that aspect of being a dragon.

"My hands . . . my fingernails changed, too." I held them up, as if they could still see the evidence of claws that had retracted hours ago.

Mom frowned. "Did those girls witness any of this?"

"No, I kept my back turned to them." I put a forkful of macaroni and cheese in my mouth.

"Good. Glad to hear it." Her brows furrowed, causing the slight wrinkles she often complained about to deepen.

Dad looked at Mom. "It's okay, Bianca. She has a good head on her shoulders. She has the instinctual dragon wisdom. She'll handle things in the right way." Dad gave me a wink and took a bite of his own macaroni and cheese.

"I'll do my best." I tried to sound enthusiastic for Mom's sake. Dad was excited, Mom was worried, and I was completely confused and overwhelmed.

"So, I assume that is just a small part of what happens when a human changes to a dragon?" I tried to sound nonchalant, although I really felt like wigging out.

"Yes. You were experiencing the beginning stages of that change." He gave me a sad smile. "This should be something you are excited about, like a rite of passage. But instead we live in a world where we have to hide these things."

I nodded again, feeling a lump in my throat. I wasn't sure I wanted to be excited about being a shifter. Especially if my being different painted a large target on my back.

Maybe this explained why Grandpa was so grumpy all the time.

# CHAPTER 5

"The ceiling needs painted." That was the first thing I said to myself as I opened my eyes Saturday morning. I didn't know why that thought popped into my head, but as I gazed upward, all I could think about was the dingy white color. Maybe this was how my brain tried to find something totally mundane to focus on. Goodness knows I'd had enough excitement to last me for months. I'd hoped to sleep in, but groaned when I turned my head to the side and saw the clock said seven a.m.

I had planned to spend my day relaxing with a book and otherwise doing a whole lot of nothing. I could have still followed through on that, so I stretched and shuffled to my bathroom. I flipped on the light and glanced at myself in the mirror, then I screamed.

Mom and Dad were in my room within moments.

"Are you okay? Where are you? What happened?" Dad shouted.

I stepped out from the bathroom and saw Dad with a baseball bat, ready to do battle. "This happened. What is this?" I asked as I held up a handful of hair.

Dad lowered the bat, and Mom's mouth formed the word "oh" without actually saying it.

"That's probably one of your special traits," Dad said as he walked toward me. "I think it looks kinda cool." He touched my hair. "Isn't this all the rage right now?"

I rolled my eyes. "It's popular to color and highlight your hair all kinds of crazy colors, yes. But I'm not sure this is the same thing." I stepped back into the bathroom and gazed at my reflection. My raven-black hair now had streaks of iridescent white dispersed throughout. The contrast was almost blinding. I turned my head and noticed that the light sparkled off the white strands. It reminded me of a pearl, with the subtle colors chasing the light as I moved.

Mom stood in the doorway. "It's rather beautiful, once you get over the shock."

I nodded. "Yeah, I guess." My mind reeled with the mockery that would come my way at school on Monday. At least I had the weekend to adjust to it. "Do you think I could dye it back to black?"

Dad's voice carried from my bedroom to the bathroom. "You could try, but my guess is that it won't take."

"Oh joy," I said. "One more reason for me to stand out."

Mom smiled at me. "One more thing that is uniquely you and completely breathtaking."

I had to refrain from rolling my eyes yet again. She was my mom. She had to say stuff like that. Instead I smiled back at her.

"Thank you." It's the only response I could muster.

By the time lunch rolled around, I'd found myself sitting in a booth at Whisper Falls Inn, thanks to my mom's orchestrations of a "surprise" visit from my best friend, who screamed with delight when she saw my hair. My black hoodie was my *new* best friend now. I would never take it off again.

"Take off that hood, Zoey!" Miranda whispered at me loudly, for the third time.

"No way," I growled. "I'm not ready to showcase this mess to the whole town. I'm still getting used to it myself."

Miranda crossed her arms and tapped her fingers with impatience. "It looks freaking amazing. I might see if my hairdresser can replicate it."

"You lie," I muttered.

"Seriously." Miranda crossed her finger over her heart. "I'm a little jealous actually. I'm usually the first one to try new styles, but Mother Nature helped you scoop me on this one."

I couldn't help but grin a little. "I don't know . . . it's just so different. Not remotely subtle. And it happened overnight. Last night I went to bed with normal, boring hair. Today . . ."

"That's part of why it's amazing. You can't help but gaze at it, like a work of art." She reached across the table that sat between us and squeezed my hand. "Now lower your hood."

I played with a small strand of dark hair that had escaped my hood. "I don't know. I'm not ready for the stares, even if they are because people think it's cool. I don't like being the center of attention."

Miranda started to say something else when Michaela, the inn owner, arrived with our food. She sat back and waited until my plate and both of our glasses were settled on the table, then took a sip of her drink. "Yum. I love this place. Thanks to Michaela, they always have my favorite drink here. She's a vampire, too, and prefers the same food source I do." Michaela winked at us before she strolled back into the kitchen, and Miranda smiled at her. "Your mom was right to suggest I take you out today. You've gotta come out of your shell a little more, and I'm just the girl to help you do it."

I groaned. "I've been an antisocial freak all my life. One afternoon with you isn't going to change that."

"No." She played with her straw. "But it will help."

I shook my head.

"Eat up. We have a full day ahead of us." She pulled out her cell phone, and I heard the clicking sound as she typed.

"Now what are you doing?" I asked.

"I'm texting my mom. I'm letting her know we are going to be in town the rest of the day and that I'm using the credit card." She flashed me an excited grin.

"I'm doomed." I pouted as I shoved a French fry in my mouth.

47

WE WALKED out of Callie's Consignments with two formal gowns in tow. I wasn't sure how I felt about the upcoming ball, but knowing that I'd be there with Jordan, I was willing to step out of my comfort zone a bit.

"You could have shopped at Dress Perfect. I wouldn't have minded at all." I felt bad that Miranda chose a consignment dress when she could have had something custom made. I, on the other hand, couldn't afford something custom and wasn't about to let her pay for it.

"No way. I love this dress!" She held up her garment bag. "I've had dresses made before. Looking with you will always be much more fun than standing around for a fitting."

I smiled. "It was fun."

"Now we need jewelry." She jumped up and down in excitement.

"Oh, I have plenty of that. In fact, you can raid my stash and see if there is anything you like."

"Really?" Her eyes widened. "You'd do that?"

I shrugged. "Why not? I can't wear it all."

"But . . ." She hesitated. "How does your dragon feel about that?"

I shrugged again. "It doesn't have a say. The human side of me is more dominant where that is concerned." I wasn't totally sure what my dragon did and didn't want, but I knew it wouldn't be upset with Miranda over borrowing a little jewelry.

"Well, if you're sure, that'd be awesome!" Her smile was infectious, and I couldn't help but smile back.

We walked to her car and placed the dresses in the back seat. After she locked up, we walked toward the shop next to Madame Tahini's—the business my dad ran for my grandfather. It seemed comical, now that I knew our secret. Wouldn't people freak if they knew that dragons owned Simple Treasures Pawn Shop?

"Is your dad working today?" asked Miranda.

I shrugged. "I'm not sure. I think so."

Her grin became mischievous. "Let's go see all the stuff people have pawned."

I laughed. "It's not like we're gonna find a hidden stash of gold or someone's deep dirty secrets."

"You never know. You can learn a lot about a person from their possessions." She gave me a sly wink.

She was right. But I wasn't sure we'd know what items belonged to whom, so it likely wouldn't do us much good. I had just reached for the door when it opened, and the bell above it tinkled loudly.

"Well, hello, Zoey. I was just coming to see you." My grandfather gave me a slight smile and leaned on his ancient cane.

"Hi, Grandpa." I turned to motion to my best friend. "Have you met Miranda Saunders?" It seemed rude not to introduce her.

He turned his gaze on her, and his look was shrewd. For a moment, I feared he would be rude. Then he spoke.

"It's nice to see you, Miranda. How is your mother?" His expression and voice both indicated his sincerity.

"She's very well. I'll tell her you asked about her. Thank you, Mr. Mills." Miranda was every bit the polite young lady she should have been.

I decided to break the brief silence. "So, why were you coming to see me?" I hoped it was for something good.

I noticed real, deep emotion behind his eyes. "I wanted to give you this. It seemed like an appropriate gift for your sweet sixteen."

He placed a large, flat velvet box in my hand.

I glimpsed up at him. "Wow, thank you, Grandpa. Do you want me to open it now?"

He nodded.

I looked at Miranda, then back at the box. The hinges were old, and the lid raised slowly as I lifted the top. Nestled inside soft blue velvet sat the most beautiful necklace I'd ever seen. It held a dainty silver chain connected to a stunning stone that was also encased in silver. Specks of colors glinted up through the glossy exterior.

"It's an opal. It was your grandmother's. She wanted you to have it." His voice hitched ever so slightly as he mentioned Grandma Christine.

"How is that possible? Grandma Christine . . . I mean . . . I never had the chance to meet her. How could it be for me?" It seemed hurtful to bring up the fact that my grandmother had passed on long before I was born, but I didn't know how else to ask the question that buzzed around in my brain.

He smiled at me. "Grandmas have a sixth sense about things." He glanced at Miranda and appeared to struggle with his next string of words. "Trust me. This was meant specifically for you." He patted my shoulder. "And it'll match perfectly with your new hair color."

I felt my eyes go so wide, I feared they'd pop out of my head. How did he know? I'd firmly pulled the hood back up after trying on the dresses, so my hair remained covered. "Thank you, Grandpa. It's lovely."

He glanced down at the necklace and smiled once more. "Yes, it'll be perfect. You should wear it to the Cold Moon Ball. That's a very special day for all of us, but especially you." He nodded at Miranda and then hobbled his way around the corner and out of sight.

"Close your mouth, Zoey. You'll catch bugs in there. Wait, do dragons eat bugs?" Her expression became thoughtful.

I turned to face her. "No, we don't eat bugs . . . as far as I know." The thought almost made me gag.

"You know, he's right. That necklace is a perfect match to your new highlights." She smiled brightly.

"Not helping," I muttered.

She nudged me and laughed. "Come on, Zoey. I promise, your hair is amazing. This necklace is amazing. *You* are amazing. Give yourself some credit."

Speechless, I pulled her in for a hug.

MONDAY MORNING ARRIVED way too soon. By the time I went to bed Sunday night, my anxiety was in a full-blown tizzy. I had convinced myself that the change in my hair would only paint a larger target on my back. I'd slept fitfully, dreaming of an odd mixture of dragons, jewelry, bugs, and bullies.

As I walked up the steps to the school, I'd convinced myself I'd be crying in the bathroom by noon. I pushed through the doors and instantly tensed, waiting for the onslaught. Instead, a decent-sized crowd gathered around someone, all of them talking and laughing. No one even noticed I'd arrived.

I decided to take advantage of that moment and sneak to my locker undetected. Just as I'd reached the combination lock, I heard Miranda yell my name. I froze, then slowly turned around.

Miranda pushed her way through the group, and they all followed her. I looked at her and dropped the backpack in my hands. Miranda was all smiles as she stepped in front of me.

She put an arm around me and looked at the rest of the students surrounding us. "Doesn't it look amazing? We decided to both go super contrasty so it'd show up better." She smiled at me. "Right? We had so much fun getting our hair colored together."

The shock hit me hard, and I couldn't respond right away. Miranda's beautiful blond hair now had dark red streaks blended in. It looked really cool, to tell the truth. Everyone else seemed to be loving it.

A chorus of voices expressed that they liked mine as well, then the bell rang, and we all scattered to our classes. Miranda and I both took our seats near the back of Mr. Zander's class. I couldn't keep my eyes off my best friend.

I leaned closer to her and whispered, "What did your mom say about your hair? Did she hate it?" I really hoped her mom had a sense of humor.

"Who do you think did it? When I told her that you were self-conscious about your new look, she was all for the idea." She looked for the page number written on the chalkboard.

"I can't believe you did this." *Mind blown.*

"Don't be silly. This is what best friends do." She patted my arm. "I knew you were worried about it, so I figured if they were gonna mock it, they'd have to mock us both. But see, I told you. Everyone loves it."

Mr. Zander interrupted us. "Zoey and Miranda, anything you'd care to share with the class?"

"No, sir," I said meekly.

"Sorry, Mr. Zander. It won't happen again." Miranda smiled at him.

He went back to writing on the chalkboard, and we went back to our textbooks. I snuck one final glance at Miranda. I'd been right. It wasn't even second period, and I was in tears, but not for the reason I'd expected.

# CHAPTER 6

*M*iranda and I sat in our usual place at lunch. We were chatting along happily when someone approached our table and stood directly in front of me. I raised my eyes to see Kai Reynolds. His six-foot-tall football physique cast a formidable shadow over my fish sticks and tater tots.

"Zoey Mills." He crossed his arms in front of him.

"That's my name." I tried to smile. Kai was kind of intimidating, and at that moment, he reminded me of my grandfather. He was also very attractive, and I couldn't tear my eyes away from his face.

"We should talk," he stated.

Miranda frowned at him. "Kai, why would you need to talk with Zoey? You don't know her."

"True, but I know *about* her." His emphasis sounded like a warning.

I looked at Miranda. She sighed. "Sit down, Kai."

He pulled out the chair in front of him, took a seat, then leaned forward on the table. "I hear you're going to the Cold Moon Ball with Jordan Woods."

"I am." I'd decided over the weekend that there was no reason to deny it, despite Katy's bullying. I didn't want Jordan to think I wasn't excited about going with him.

"You should reconsider," said Kai.

"Why?" Miranda blurted out the question before I did.

He focused his golden-brown eyes on her and raised a dark eyebrow.

"Oh lord. Really? Tell me you're kidding." She shot him a glare.

He leaned back in his chair. "Mixing with humans is never a good idea."

"What?" I squeaked. I looked at Miranda, and I'm sure she saw the horror on my face.

She held up one hand. "I didn't tell him. Some supes just know."

"Are you . . ." I didn't know how to phrase the question.

"I'm like Miranda," he stated.

"I see." I really hoped one of these days I'd be one of those that "just know." I was tired of all the surprises.

"If you really want to go to the ball with someone, I can take you." He didn't crack a smile.

Miranda leaned forward. "Wow. That's a convincing way to ask a girl out. I'm surprised your flowery words haven't melted Zoey right here in her seat."

He glared at her, then moved his gaze back to me. "If not me, we can find you a suitable date, but I think we'd suit well."

My heart beat rapidly. There was something about him that kept me riveted. It was more than just his looks, but I couldn't put my finger on it, and I couldn't seem to escape it.

Sanity reentered my brain. I shook my head. "No, thank you. I've already told him I'd go with him. And for the record, I don't care if he's human or not. I like him."

He stared at me for a few seconds, then shook his head in disgust. "You're just like your dad."

I stood. "Thank you," I whispered loudly. "My dad is a great man, and I'm proud to be his daughter."

Miranda stood and put her arm around me to show her support.

Kai frowned. "You'll regret this, Zoey. It never ends well with humans."

I shrugged. "It's my mistake to make."

I didn't truly believe it was a mistake. My mom and dad were perfectly happy together.

He smirked at me. "Whatever."

He stood and walked away. I struggled to tamp down the disappointment I felt when he dismissed me so easily. *Why do I care what he thinks?*

I turned to Miranda. "What was that all about?"

She sighed and motioned for me to sit back down. She took her chair as I sat in mine. "So, Kai is a bit of a speciesist. He thinks, at the minimum, that supernaturals should only associate with other supernaturals. If he's being particularly snobby, he'll insist that most supernaturals should stick to their own specific species." She paused a moment and glanced across the room to where Kai now sat with his friends. "I think he might like you a bit, though, and would bend his species rule if you showed interest in him."

My heart lodged in my throat once more. He was so different than Jordan. Arrogant, self-assured, with a sensual vibe surrounding him. It pulled at me, and I hated myself for feeling that way.

"If that's how he talks to girls he likes, I'll pass. My grandpa is the same way, which is why he and my mom don't talk much." I hoped I sounded more convincing than I felt. I looked at my lunch, but found I'd lost my appetite.

"Either way, don't let him bother you. Only a small group in town feel the way he and your grandfather do." She took a sip from her thermos, and I wondered how my life had gone from dull to complicated so quickly.

Once home from school, I sat in my room and thought about the upcoming ball and my birthday. While I didn't truly believe what Kai said earlier in the day, it did plant a seed of doubt in my mind. I wasn't expecting marriage or anything, but I did hope that Jordan and I could at least give dating a shot.

Kai was an enigma. I understood my attraction to Jordan. He was cute, kind, and everything I'd ever thought I wanted in a guy. But I had no idea why Kai had become a contender for my feelings. I'd never been one of those girls that chased after the bad boy, and he was very much a bad boy.

"Ugh." I groaned, shaking off the frustration as I moved to my bed and sat down. I grabbed the ornate jewelry box from my nightstand and placed it in my lap so I could study the maze of lines on the top, as I had so many times before. This time, when I traced the lines with my fingers, they moved.

"What the heck?" I watched in disbelief as the metal changed shape. "I knew this was special. I knew it!" I couldn't contain my excitement.

Once the pieces stopped moving, I noticed an empty circular spot in the center. I leaned closer to get a better look and grandma's necklace, which hung around my neck, gravitated to it like a magnet. *No way! It couldn't be!*

With great care, I reached behind my neck and unclasped the chain, letting the pendant fall completely into the center of the lid. The lines on the top moved around once more, and a small compartment in the side popped open.

"Whoa. The necklace is a key."

I pulled the compartment drawer the rest of the way out and found a letter inside. With shaky hands, I removed the paper and unfolded it. The fragile parchment had yellowed with time. After placing the jewelry box on the bed, I carefully straightened the letter out in my lap.

*Dear Granddaughter,*

*I know this will come as a surprise, but I knew you would be the one to own the box and the necklace. How did I know? Well, let's just say that not all fortune tellers are frauds. Speaking of which, please tell Madame Tahini thank you for her wisdom and advice. Without her, I would not have known to write you.*

*While I do not know your name, I do have a somewhat detailed description of what you look like. You are almost at your sixteenth birthday, and lots of changes are ahead. Some have already happened; others are yet to come. Embrace who you are, little one. Be proud of your heritage. You come from an extensive line of Icelandic Frost Dragons who once roamed the earth in mighty droves before the human population vastly increased. We are still a noble species with much to offer those around us. Most of us are wise beyond our years, although at times, I wonder if your stubborn grandfather isn't the exception to the rule. We possess amazing gifts as well. Some are universal; others are unique to each dragon. You'll learn what yours are as you mature.*

*Never fear, little one; you are stronger than you know. Never back down from doing what is right, and always act in kindness and compassion. This will never steer you wrong.*

*Take great care with this necklace. Opals are known for their magic properties, but this one is extra special. It contains a spell that will help you control the emotions that come with growing up as a shifter. It will also help you with any specific needs you may struggle with. What those will be, I can't say—only the stone knows. Some days you'll feel like more of a dragon, others you'll feel more human. Eventually both sides must coexist in harmony if you choose to stay in Havenwood Falls. That's a choice only you can make, once you're of age. Choose wisely, my granddaughter, and know you are loved.*

*Grandma Christine*


*P.S.: I love the white in your hair. Never change that.*


"Whoa. This is too much to handle." I carefully placed the letter on the jewelry box and moved it to my nightstand. I closed my eyes as I flopped myself back onto the bed. It blew my mind to think my grandmother knew a lot of what would come to be. Her words sunk into my heart and warmed my soul. A tear slid down my cheek as I realized that I missed her, and I'd never even met her. But she seemed to know me, and I think we would have gotten along wonderfully.

My grandfather was a totally different story. I didn't know how to take him. I believed that Grandma served as a cushion that softened Grandpa's blows. But now she was gone, he was angry, and I was sure I had missed a vital part of that puzzle.

# CHAPTER 7

*a*larm. Clothes. Breakfast. The following day started out fairly normal. Well, as normal as it can be for someone who was half dragon. I did my best to keep my head down, focus on work, and not be noticed. I'd just stepped outside the school doors when Jordan approached me.

"Hey, Zoey." He smiled, and my insides began to melt.

"Hi, Jordan." I did my best to look confident and return his smile.

He slipped his arms through his backpack and shifted the weight so it rested on his shoulders. "I like the new hair color. It's . . . unique."

I couldn't tell if he really liked it, or if it was simply kindness on his part. "Thanks. I wanted to try something different."

"You succeeded. It looks great on you." He continued to smile at me, and I tried to focus less on that and more on his words.

I looked down at my feet for a moment, hoping the rush of heat to my cheeks would quickly subside. "I'm glad you like it."

He stuck his hands in his pockets. "So, I was wondering if you had any plans tonight?"

I shook my head. "I don't think so. I'd have to check with my parents to be sure."

"Would you like to grab pizza with me? I thought we could go to Napoli's." He appeared to be a little nervous, and it was endearing.

"Yeah, sure. That'd be nice." I struggled to keep the tremble from my voice. I had to play it cool. It wouldn't do to scare him off before I even had a chance to know him.

"Great. I'll pick you up around five thirty then, if that's okay."

I nodded. "That'd be perfect."

He turned and jogged down the steps while I stood there, grinning like an idiot.

I reached up and ran my fingers over my grandmother's necklace, which brought me comfort. Maybe it was the connection to my grandmother. Or maybe the spell contained in the stone. I didn't really know what brought about the soothing of my soul. All I could be sure of was that the necklace and I were fated to belong to one another.

My dad pulled up in front of the school, and I quickly made my way to the car. After strapping in, I wasted no time in finding out the evening plans.

"Are we doing anything special tonight?" I kept my voice casual.

"Just the norm. Why? Have plans?" He grinned at me.

"I do, if it's okay. Jordan asked me to grab pizza with him tonight." I pressed my lips together, trying to contain my enthusiasm.

"Ah, I see. Sounds fun. Do you need a ride?" He kept his eyes on the road.

"No, he's picking me up," I said as I dug through my backpack to be sure I'd packed my geography homework.

"Glad to hear it. It'll finally give me a chance to do the protective dad routine I've been practicing since I learned you were gonna be a girl." We pulled up to a stoplight, and he rubbed his hands together like a villain from some corny superhero show.

"Dad, please. Don't embarrass me." I felt sure I'd expire from utter humiliation if he did anything crazy.

"Me?" he asked, his voice full of surprise and innocence.

"Yes, you." I pointed a finger at him. "You love pushing your dad boundaries. I can deal with the dad jokes, but antics like cleaning a gun in front of my date is too far."

He shook his head. "I don't even own a gun, sweetheart. I do, however, own knives. Lots of knives."

"Dad . . ." I said in warning.

He laughed the rest of the way to our street. I, on the other hand, contemplated the logistics of running away from home.

~

JORDAN and I sat in a booth at Napoli's with a large cheese pizza between us. I'd debated how I should dress, but after a long argument with myself, the sensible side of my personality won, and I opted for a clean pair of jeans and a nice, but not too fancy blouse. Jordan had changed as well and looked amazing in his jeans and blue polo shirt.

"This pizza is so good," I murmured just before taking a bite of my second slice.

"It's the best." He took a bite of his own and winked at me.

"You said you've lived here all your life. Do you like it?" I thought that a safe place to start a conversation about his life.

"Yes and no. Like all small towns, it has its pros and cons." He took a sip of his cola.

"Football team, lots of friends . . . I'm gonna guess the good outweighs the bad. You've got it made here." I teased him, but his eyes were somber.

"Don't be so sure. School isn't everything. We've discussed moving a couple of times, but it never worked out. I used to get frustrated by that, but now . . . Well, I'm glad I'm still here."

I tried not to blush. "I'm glad, too."

He reached across the table and took my hand in his. "I know we don't know each other very well, but there is just something about you that I'm drawn to. You're not like most of the other girls here."

*Dude, you have no idea.* "Oh, I'm pretty average. Nothing special about me."

"See, there's where you're wrong. Besides being unusually pretty, there is something about you that I can't put my finger on. Something deep on the inside that is dying to come out." He rubbed his thumb over the back of my hand, and goosebumps raced down my spine. If he only knew how close to the truth he really was. Yet I'm not sure he could ever know. Kai's words pricked at the back of my mind. His face invaded my thoughts, and I had to push the image away.

"I know that sounds like a tacky pickup line," he said, "but it's the honest truth. I don't know how else to explain it."

"Thank you. That's very sweet." I hoped my face expressed how much his words truly meant. I didn't feel so much like an outsider in that moment.

"I've gotta hit the restroom. I'll be right back." He scooted out of the booth and headed to the back of the restaurant. I'd just taken another bite of pizza when Kai sat down in Jordan's seat.

"I've warned you about Jordan. Why won't you listen?" He was annoyed, and the frown he wore was severe.

I reached up and touched my necklace. "No, you told me it was a bad idea, but you never really said why."

I was really getting tired of people trying to tell me what to do. I crossed my arms and stared him down, begging my emotions not to betray me. They didn't listen. My skin prickled with awareness as Kai reached across the table and placed his hand over mine.

His voice changed and became tender. "You will never have the normal life he'll expect. Things will happen. You'll change." He leaned back against the seat. "How are you gonna explain the first time you change into a full-blown dragon in front of him? Think he'll just laugh it off?"

I shrugged. "I don't know, Kai. It's not like we're engaged. We're just hanging out. Take a Xanax and calm down."

"My, you're certainly becoming outspoken," he sneered.

"How would you know? Outside of my secret, you know me even less than Jordan."

His eyes bored into mine. "I'm giving you fair warning. End it. You should be with me. Don't make this harder than it has to be." He stood and walked away as if he hadn't just threatened me.

"Jerk," I muttered as I looked back down at my pizza and tried to slow my fluttering heartbeat. He was correct about one thing—I did suddenly gain an attitude that wasn't my norm. I didn't know where this confidence came from, but I liked it. The necklace again? Possibly. I wished the necklace could tell me why Kai and Jordan both appealed to me, and which one was the correct choice.

Within minutes of Kai leaving, Jordan made it back to our table. "Sorry I took so long. I also had to call and check on my mom."

"No need to apologize. I think it's great that you care for her so much. Is she ill?" I hoped I wasn't being intrusive.

"Uh, yeah . . . sorta. She wasn't feeling well when I left earlier." He seemed to have lost interest in his pizza.

"Do you need to be with her? I don't mind if you need to go." I'd be disappointed, but family was important.

He fidgeted in his seat and began to look uncomfortable. "I don't want to go, but I should probably check on her in person."

I nodded. "Sure, we can try this again later. And there is always the ball." I smiled to reassure him that I wasn't in the least upset.

"Thank you." He quickly left his seat and went to the register to pay the bill. While I waited, the waitress came over and boxed up the remaining slices of pizza to go.

He returned, I picked up the box, and we walked side by side to his car. We'd just buckled up when his cell phone buzzed. He pulled it out and frowned. "Hey, do you mind if we make a quick stop before I take you home?"

"No, not at all." I couldn't help but be concerned by the way his face drained of color.

He put the car in gear, and we sped down the street toward the south end of the town square. It wasn't a far drive, but we arrived at our destination faster than I'd have thought humanly possible.

We pulled up to Building B in an apartment complex called Havenwood Village. He slammed the car into park and turned to me. "Stay here. I'll be right back."

Before I had a chance to respond, he bolted out the door and took the steps two at a time. I saw him enter an apartment with the number 204 on the door. I sat quietly waiting, when I heard a loud crash. I forgot all about his request to stay, and I bounded up the stairs after him.

When I pushed open the door to the apartment, I found Jordan hunched over a woman lying on the floor. He sat her upright. Blood dripped from her mouth, and a bruise covered her cheek.

"I'm here, Mom. I'm here," he soothed as he pulled her close to him.

"Jordan? Is everything okay?" I wanted to help, although in truth I felt totally helpless.

His eyes snapped to mine. "No, thank you. I thought you were going to wait in the car." He sounded a little angry.

"I was, but then I heard a crash, and it worried me."

His eyes drifted to a spot on the opposite wall where the remains of a lamp lay in pieces.

"It's nothing I can't take care of." Ice laced his words, and I realized I was completely out of place. I was an intruder, and he didn't want me there.

"Okay, sorry. I'll just go back downstairs." I turned and carefully made my way down the steps and to his car. I struggled with the idea of waiting on him or calling my parents. In the end, I settled on walking home. As I crossed the town square, I spotted the gazebo. I was drawn to it, and before I realized what I had done, I found myself seated just inside the latticework.

The chill in the air surrounded me, yet once again I found I didn't really need a coat or my hoodie, though I wore it anyway. Normally, I'd have been shivering by now. This dragon trait made me immensely grateful in that moment. I hated being cold.

Jordan's red Toyota slowed to a stop at the curb across from me. He got out and cautiously walked toward me. I wasn't sure if I should be worried or mad. He behaved like a jerk back there, and I only tried to help. Kai's face flashed in my mind, and I pushed it away for the second time that night.

Jordan reached the railing and leaned against it. "Hi."

I looked up at him, a frown creasing my face. "Hi."

I had no enthusiasm left to give at the moment. First Kai, and now this. I was tired.

"I'm sorry about that back there. I'm not used to . . . I mean, not many people know about . . . that." He fidgeted and kicked the tip of his tennis shoe in the dirt.

"I won't tell anyone. I'm not a gossip." It hurt that he might not trust me.

63

"I know. It's not that." He stepped up onto the wooden flooring and walked to stand beside me. "Can I sit?"

I motioned to the empty spot beside me.

He perched his butt on the edge and crossed his legs out in front of him. "My dad hits my mom. I can't stop it."

I could hear the distress that admission caused him.

"I'm so sorry, Jordan. I don't know how you'd stop something like that. Can you call the police?" I hoped I wasn't asking a stupid question.

He shook his head. "The first time I did, Mom lied and told them that she'd fallen down the stairs. She had bruises on her arms from where she'd tried to block his blows. That was just a minor one." He sighed. "She wouldn't press charges or tell the truth, so I knew it was a waste of time after that."

"Why not?" I asked, then realized I probably knew why. For the same reason I didn't want to pursue Katy and her friends after they hit me. I feared it would only get worse.

"She loves the jerk. And I think she's afraid he'd kill her once he got out of jail." He turned to me with tears in his eyes. "He will, ya know. He'll kill her. And me, too. He's only hit me once, and that time my mom lost it on him, but it didn't change anything. Now I work to keep the peace as much as possible. I can tell when he's had a bad day, so I check on her if I'm not home. She didn't answer the phone, so I knew something was wrong."

My heart broke for him. I couldn't imagine living in that kind of environment—seeing someone you love hurting someone else you love. No one deserved that.

I reached over and took his hand. "Don't feel guilty. You are doing all you know to do." I swallowed. "If you ever need someone to talk to, or just want to get away for a bit, feel free to call me. It'd be a privilege to be there for you." He nodded, but I wanted more. I wanted a smile. "Wow, now who's using the cheesy pickup lines?"

He smiled then, and my heart almost stopped beating. I did that. I caused that beautiful smile in a sad moment.

He sat back on the bench a little and adjusted so he faced me, then he leaned forward, and before I knew what happened, he kissed me. At some point, I must have closed my eyes, because I had to open them to look into his.

He smiled and ran a finger down my cheek. "You really are amazing, Zoey. I'm so glad I know you."

I shivered at his touch. "I'm glad I know you, too." This time I closed the gap between us, and I had the first real, heart-stopping kiss I'd ever experienced.

# CHAPTER 8

*J*ordan continued to kiss me. A thrill ran through me as his lips touched mine over and over. His hands began to roam over my body, and while I liked his touch, I knew this pushed the limits for a first date. I kept my eyes closed and pushed his hands to my back, where they belonged. He moved them to explore my body once again, this time with more force, and my eyes flew open to protest, then I screamed.

I wasn't kissing Jordan. I was kissing Kai! His seductive smile and bedroom eyes pulled me in. I didn't want to want him, but I did. He put one hand in my hair and pulled my head back, giving him access to my neck. He kissed lightly, and I couldn't stop the groan that escaped my lips.

He moved to my ear and whispered, "See, Zoey? See how it could be between us? Don't fight it."

Knocking interrupted yet another passionate kiss. He pulled back and whispered, "Go away."

The knocking continued, so this time I repeated his words, but louder. "Go away."

"Zoey? Are you up yet? We have a busy day ahead of us."

*Mom? Why is Mom here?*

The knocking became louder.

I bolted up in bed and rubbed my face. Mom knocked on my bedroom door again, then opened it.

"You need to get around, sleepyhead. We have so much to do before the Cold Moon Ball tomorrow." She winked at me, then closed the door behind her.

*A dream? Oh, thank God it was a dream.* The tension drained from my body. I really hated that I'd dreamed about Jordan and Kai had forced his way in. Jordan and I had only gone on the one date, but it felt like I had cheated on him. We weren't officially an item yet, so cheating wasn't really an issue, but after last night's kiss, I'd hoped there was a future for us. If only I could get Kai out of my head.

I quickly dressed and went to the kitchen to help. Everyone worked on prepping for the celebrations that would follow on Sunday. Even my mom jumped in on the action by baking pies for the huge meal that preceded the ball.

The doorbell rang just as I had intended to ask Mom what she needed me to do.

"Saved by the bell," I quipped. Then I yelled down the hall as I walked to the front door, "I'll get it."

I swung it open to find Aunt Jetta standing on the other side.

"Hey, kiddo! How are you?" I hadn't even said hello when she pushed her way in and started touching my hair. "Oh my gosh. This is gorgeous! I wish my hair would have done this."

I laughed. "Yeah, it's been an attention-getter, all right."

She hugged me and looked down into my face. "Seriously though, how are you? Are you handling all this change okay?"

I nodded. "For the most part. I'm learning to be okay with it."

"I'm glad to hear it. Would you like to have a girls' day out—just you and me? It would let us get acquainted better." The excitement in her features rubbed off on me, and I realized I really did want to go.

"I would, but I feel like I should help with the Cold Moon stuff." I tried to hide my disappointment. I liked Aunt Jetta. She oozed fun from every pore.

"Nah, don't worry about that. Everyone has it covered. And since tomorrow is also your birthday, I thought it'd be good to do something special today. Something I think you need to see."

"Oh, okay. Let me check with Mom." I turned to see Mom walking up behind us.

"Yes, you should go. Aunt Jetta will take good care of you, and I'll see you back here tonight." She wiped her hands on a dish towel.

"Seriously? You don't want me to work and learn all about the process of doing for others?" My sarcasm did not go unnoticed, but it did surprise me how easily she was willing to let me off the hook.

"Seriously. You've learned that plenty. It's not every year you get a Cold Moon Ball and your sixteenth birthday all in one day. There are other lessons to learn today." She looked at Aunt Jetta, and it felt like an unspoken message passed between them.

"Okay then," I said. "What do I need to wear?"

Aunt Jetta smiled. "Something very comfortable and loose."

*Loose? Well, this should be good.*

I jogged to my room and quickly changed into a pair of sweatpants, T-shirt with hoodie, and my favorite tennis shoes. In less than ten minutes, I had returned to the doorway with Mom and Aunt Jetta.

"Okie dokie. I'm all set. Teach me, oh master," I said with a mock bow.

Aunt Jetta chuckled and motioned for me to exit the doorway before her. I did, but not before turning to give my mom a big hug. "I love you," I whispered.

"I love you, too," she whispered back and planted a kiss in my hair.

WE'D BEEN HIKING up the side of a ridge in the woods outside of town for almost an hour. My legs grew tired, and I realized how badly I needed to start a cardio routine of some kind. Aunt Jetta moved ahead of me with ease.

"Hurry up, slowpoke. I have something cool to show you." She waved me forward.

I huffed in annoyance. "I'm coming."

She waited until I reached the spot where she stood and let me catch my breath. "Look."

I raised my eyes, and my mouth fell open. Before me stood a gorgeous waterfall—three, actually. They weren't tall, not like the great falls the town was named for. The water had partially frozen, but I hadn't noticed the cold. Again, my dragon kept me comfortable. With each day, I started to like my dragon more and more.

"This is called Small's Falls. Isn't it beautiful?" Aunt Jetta placed her hands on her hips and gazed at the falls with a fondness in her eyes that I'd not previously seen before.

"It is beautiful. Is this a special place?" I studied her face.

"It is. Very much so. How did you know?" She moved next to me and put an arm around me.

"The look on your face. You seem happy to see it." It embarrassed me a little to admit I was so in tune with her expressions. It seemed odd to be so familiar with her, considering I didn't know her that well.

"It will soon be a special place for you, too." She gave me a brief squeeze before she stepped aside. "Follow me."

I stretched a moment, then fell in step behind her. We walked in silence, the only sounds being the occasional animal running to avoid crossing paths with us, or the crunch of leaves and frost under our feet.

As we approached the falls, she stopped, clearing the overgrown path in front of her. "Wow, it's been a while since anyone has been here. We'll be changing that."

I watched her pull dead vines and various small branches out of the way as we walked. We stopped, and she pointed out a very narrow outcropping of rocks that trailed down the small cliff connecting to the falls. She stepped out onto one, and my heart stopped.

"What are you doing? That looks dangerous." I felt my anxiety creep up, and I reached to touch my opal, then realized I'd left it at home. I feared losing it in the mountains.

"It's okay, Zoey. I know the steps don't look like much, but not everything is as it appears. Come here." She motioned for me to take her hand.

I slowly approached her, and she grasped my hand in hers. "Do you trust me?"

Fear robbed me of my voice, but I also felt sure Aunt Jetta would never put me in danger. I nodded.

"Good. Hang on to my hand tightly." She squeezed my hand for reassurance. Before I knew what happened, she yanked me toward her and down on the ledge.

My heart felt like it'd leapt into my throat. I looked down at the tiny ledge we stood on, only it wasn't tiny. It was more like a landing than a ledge. Plenty of room for both of us.

"See? It's an optical illusion. You can't see the steps until you're right up on them." She winked at me.

"Cool." I gazed down to see several larger steps that led all the way to the bottom of the falls.

"Okay, ready to see something really awesome?" Her enthusiasm once again spread over me.

"I am." I still reeled a little in shock over the freaky stairs, but I did my best to push past that.

I followed her to the bottom, where we were close enough to the water to feel the occasional splash. She turned to me and took my hand once more, leading me to a door-sized opening in the rock. She pulled a small flashlight from her pocket and clicked it on. With two quick steps, she moved inside and was completely swallowed by the darkness.

"Aunt Jetta? Where'd you go?" I willed myself to remain calm. "I can't see you."

As if by magic, her arm thrust through the darkness. "Take my hand again. It'll make sense once you're inside."

I grabbed hold of her with both hands and let her lead me through the curtain of inky blackness. It surrounded me like a thick obsidian fog, and then suddenly we were in a small cave, her flashlight illuminating most of the room.

"How . . . I mean . . . I couldn't see the light from outside." I moved my gaze from the room to the dark doorway.

"It's witchcraft." She wiggled her eyebrows up and down at me, and I rolled my eyes.

"No, really," I said, "how does it work?"

"I wasn't kidding. It's witchcraft. The Luna Coven has helped us keep this cave a secret. It's all ours." She gestured around us. "And you haven't even seen the best part."

"Really? It's our cave?" I walked closer to her.

"Yep. Let me show you the main room." She shined the light in the direction of a larger opening, and from where I stood, I could see tiny specks of light.

"What is that?" Curiosity won out over fear, and I moved forward.

Aunt Jetta walked right behind me. We passed through the opening, and she pulled out a lighter. She held it up, and that's when I saw the torches lining the wall. I watched her light each one until the entire room became bathed in a flickering amber light.

Once more, she shone her flashlight on the opposite wall, and it sparkled. "Go take a closer look," she urged.

I slowly walked forward while she kept the light focused in front of me. When I reached the wall, I extended my hand and ran my fingers over the rough texture. It was comprised of dirt and rock, but something else pushed through—something embedded within.

"That's kimberlite." She watched me as I ruffled through my memories. I'd heard that name somewhere before, but I couldn't place it.

I turned to look at her. "I don't get it."

"Diamonds. Kimberlite contains diamonds." She spoke calmly, but I could see the elation in her eyes.

"No way!" I hopped up and down a bit. "We own all these diamonds?"

"We do. How do you think we pay for our lifestyle? The pawn shop hasn't been *that* lucrative. Although to be fair, your Grandpa Mills was a whiz with investments. So, he's probably earned as much as we've pulled from this cave."

"Whoa." I couldn't believe its beauty.

"There's more." She motioned for me to follow her once again.

We approached another opening and stepped through. She lit a few more torches while I stayed in place. When she lit the last one, she turned to me. "Ta da."

I looked around and gasped. "This cave is *huge*."

"It is. And look at that end." She pointed in a direction, I didn't know which since I'd lost my bearings inside the cave, and I walked

71

toward it, noticing a light at the end. The closer I approached, the lighter it became. I could also hear water running.

"We're behind the falls?" *Way cool!*

"We are," she said. "And again, no one can get in here. Just us dragons."

"People don't stumble upon it by accident?" I asked.

"A few have, but the spell protects it. All anyone else can see is a small, dark, and empty cave. Pretty cool, huh?"

I nodded. Beyond cool. Simply amazing.

She sat down on a large rock. "Humans have learned to avoid it all together. The water is fatal to them."

"So. Cool."

She motioned to me to join her. "Zoey, we need to talk."

*That phrase is never good.*

"Okay." I made my way next to her and sat down.

"Being a dragon shifter can take some getting used to. The hardest part is making the transition from human to dragon. It's something you have to practice the first few times." She reached down and clasped my hand. "It's not as scary as it sounds, but it's not something you can just practice out in the open. This cave gives us plenty of room for that."

"Oh. So, this is our training space." I suddenly worried about the pain that might be involved in shifting. It wasn't something I'd considered before.

"Yes, exactly. I brought you here today to practice." Her tone held excitement.

"What?" I jumped up. "I'm not ready for that. My birthday isn't until tomorrow." I started to panic again.

"Sweetheart, you could have shifted anytime you wanted to this past couple of weeks. You just didn't know how." She clasped her hands in front of her.

I looked at her and took a deep breath. "Does it hurt?"

She shrugged. "It can be a little uncomfortable for your human form, but nothing you can't handle. I promise."

I nodded, still a bit apprehensive. "Okay."

"Let me help you. I'll explain how you do it, then I'll change. You can follow me."

I nodded again.

"So first, you take off your clothes, unless you want to be without wearable clothes when you return to your human form." She started stripping, and I focused my view on the dirt in front of me. "Zoey, don't let this embarrass you. It's part of the process. Animals don't wear clothes, and they aren't embarrassed to see each other. You shouldn't be, either. At least, not in this instance." She folded up her clothing and placed them on the rock she had just sat on. "Now look at me."

I looked up and tried to focus on her face. Even though I shouldn't have been embarrassed, I was.

"Think of your dragon. Talk to it. Allow it to come forward in your mind. Once you've freed it in your thoughts, you'll be able to free it physically, too. Now watch."

She stood back and closed her eyes. Within moments she began to change shape before my eyes. She groaned a little, but it didn't sound like she suffered. Her hands became huge claws with long talons while her arms morphed into muscular legs that jutted out in front of her. Her legs followed a similar pattern. Her head thrashed back and changed from the face I was now familiar with to one of a giant, fierce reptile. A crown of thorny looking scales wrapped from one side of her jaw to the other. Powerful wings poked out from her shoulder blades, and her tail grew to almost the length of her body. Aunt Jetta's scales were white with a blueish tint to match her eyes. Snout to tail, she had to be forty feet long and twenty feet high. She opened her mighty jaws and I saw the gleam of enormous teeth. Some were smooth like fangs, while others featured a serrated edge. She was beautiful and terrifying all at once.

I took a few steps back, and she gently placed her monstrous head in front of me. I reached out and touched her snout. "Aunt Jetta?"

She snorted, and frosty air rushed from her nostrils. I recognized it, as it looked like the same stuff I blew on my burn that fateful day I learned about my true identity.

She blinked one large, pale blue reptilian eye at me and gave my hand a small nudge.

I instantly felt less afraid. "Okay, I'll do it."

I stood back and took off my clothes, trying to concentrate on anything but the fact that I was naked in a half-frozen cave. I closed my eyes and tried to imagine what my dragon might look like. A vision began to form in my mind. A white dragon with iridescent scales stepped forward and bowed to me. I bowed back and reached forward to touch it. It lowered its head and allowed me to stroke its magnificent crown.

"Are you my dragon?" I asked. It nodded its head. "Will you promise to keep me safe?"

It nodded once again.

I stepped closer and wrapped my arms around its neck in an embrace. I could feel the affection my dragon had for my human form, and all my fears dissipated. In seconds, we were melding together. I felt my muscles and bones expanding and pulling, but it wasn't horrible. Along with a little pain, it felt like finally getting a good stretch after a long nap. My bones creaked slightly, and I felt some popping.

When I mustered the courage to open my eyes, I was looking up, only slightly, at my Aunt Jetta. She spoke to me, and I felt relief that we could still communicate in this form, albeit telepathically.

"You're beautiful, Zoey. One of the most beautiful dragons I've ever seen." She pushed her head against mine and rubbed our cheeks together.

"Am I?" I wished I had a mirror.

"How do you feel?" she asked.

"A little weird, but good. Really good." I felt like smiling, although I had to assume that I couldn't physically smile. Maybe human Zoey smiled for me, somewhere inside.

"Do you feel like getting some exercise?" She stamped her feet for emphasis. "I'm dying to stretch out my wings."

"Can we do that? I thought you said we shouldn't be seen outside of the cave." I wiggled my wings a little, testing how they felt. I could only move them minutely, thanks to the now cramped space in the cave.

"That's true. But we have one more trick up our sleeves.

Camouflage." She lifted one front leg and pointed a claw at the falls at the end of the cave. "We can exit that way."

She lumbered past me, and I awkwardly followed, still getting used to walking on four large legs. She pushed her head through the water of the falls and then back inside, shaking the water off like a dog would after a bath. "We're good. We'll step out into the water, then I'll show you how to trigger your camouflage."

She pushed her way through the falls, with me close behind her. We both sat in roughly knee-deep water. Well, knee deep for a twenty-foot-tall creature. I glanced down at my rippled reflection in the water. As she'd said, beautiful. I now stared back at the dragon I'd envisioned in my mind. My coloring was pure as snow, with iridescent scales that matched the streaks in my human form's hair. My eyes were more a marbled grey and contained even less blue than my human form did. My crown of horns mimicked Jetta's, but was smaller, as was the rest of my sizing. I turned my head and opened my jaw, inspecting the copious number of teeth that now filled my mouth.

"See? You're stunning." She stepped a bit closer. "When you're a full adult, at age twenty, you'll be the same size as I am. You're not all that far from it now. I'd estimate you're close to sixteen or seventeen feet tall."

I looked back at my reflection in awe.

"So," she said, "to hide within your surroundings, simply scan the area around you and mentally choose a camouflage. Your body will do the rest."

She stepped onto the bank, and I followed her. She glanced around us, then disappeared. But she wasn't completely gone. I could sense her and see little things that gave her away, but I felt sure that was another perk to being a dragon. We could still see each other, for the most part, but others couldn't.

I followed her lead. I didn't feel different, but when I looked at my claws, they appeared transparent. I could still see them, yet I couldn't. It felt surreal.

Jetta stretched her wings out and sighed in bliss. "It's been so long." She shifted her head toward mine. "Are you ready for more?"

I couldn't help but be excited. "Yes. Totally."

"Good. Let's fly."

# CHAPTER 9

$\mathcal{I}$ followed Aunt Jetta to a higher altitude, practicing my camouflage techniques along the way. I could shift from dead leaves to snow, to trees, to water, and back again. I could even make one part of myself resemble the trees, while another part of me looked like the ground. I loved it. We were totally undetectable, outside of the sounds we made as we traversed the mountainside. Even then I was surprised at how nimble we could be for such large creatures. We weren't nearly as noisy as I'd expected we'd be.

We reached a cliff, and she stopped to face the open air that stretched out in front of us. I could see the entire town from where we were perched.

"It's beautiful," I whispered.

"It truly is." She turned her head toward me and pushed her forehead to mine in an affectionate gesture. "I hope you'll give it a chance, Zoey. Havenwood Falls is an amazing place, once you settle in."

I nodded as I pulled my face from hers.

"I'd miss you if you left, but I'd also understand." Aunt Jetta spoke softly in my mind. "Your grandpa can be a tyrant when he doesn't get his way. He can make life very difficult, if he chooses to."

"I have no plans to leave. Not at the moment. I guess time will tell."

"Good." She nodded in front of us. "Then let's get a closer look." She moved to the edge and stepped off into nothingness.

My breath hitched as I waited for her to reemerge in my sightline. Then suddenly she appeared, hovering just above me, flapping her beautiful wings with a grace I could only hope to achieve.

"It's easy," she yelled. "Just step off and flap your wings. Instinct will take over."

Falling terrified me. I moved to the edge and looked down. It had to be hundreds of feet to the bottom. I felt my claws dig into the earth of their own will, grasping at anything that would pull me from the edge. Instead, I'd managed to mangle the earth beneath me until it gave way, and I fell.

Screaming as I plunged to the earth, I frantically tried to remember what Aunt Jetta had instructed. The wind rushed past my face, and my eyes couldn't focus as dirt, rocks, and trees passed my vision at a breakneck pace. Without effort, my wings extended fully, and I flapped them in a panic. It wasn't elegant or delicate, but it kept me from colliding with the rocks below.

I slowly rose into the air, trying to gain my bearings while I worked to smooth my rhythm. Aunt Jetta swooped down beside me, then shot back up into the air like a rocket, her body spinning like a top as she passed through the clouds.

I wanted to do that. I wanted to soar and dive and swoop. I flew up to where she'd disappeared and hovered in place as I searched for her. "Aunt Jetta! Where are you?"

She glided next to me, as if she were swimming in the air. "I'm here, sweetie."

"I want to do all of that. All of it!"

She laughed. "You will, just follow my lead."

She pointed her head down, tucked in her legs and pulled her wings tight against her back. She bolted like a rocket.

I repeated her motions, and in seconds, the ground rushed up to meet me. It was exhilarating! As we neared the ground we both extended our wings, and they worked like a parachute, slowing our descent. We flapped a few times, and once again we were rising about the trees.

I continued to lift, letting all my stress and worries slip away. This brought peace. This was heaven. I lost track of time as I practiced gliding across the sky, enjoying a freedom I'd never felt before.

Aunt Jetta landed on an outcropping of rocks, and I settled in beside her.

"It's an amazing feeling, isn't it?" she murmured.

"It is. It's my new favorite thing." I couldn't keep the awe from my voice. I reveled in this newfound ability.

"Something you need to know, Zoey. Don't lose yourself too much as you fly. If your dragon gains too much control, your human side may never return."

I blinked several times as I tried to comprehend what she meant. "I might stay a dragon forever?"

"Only if you truly choose it. And in this day and age, sometimes it seems the better choice. But never forget that there are wonders to your human side, too. Things you would miss, and people who would miss you."

I nodded. "I promise to be careful."

"Good." She stretched her wings once more. "We should probably head back. Tomorrow is a big day."

My time with Aunt Jetta yesterday had been amazing. I'd learned that shifting back required a similar process as before. I had to embrace my alter ego each time.

December third had finally arrived—my sixteenth birthday and the day of the Cold Moon Ball. Everyone ran around like mad, setting up for the various festivities that would begin around dinner time. I helped my dad set up the tables inside the Annex, which is where the party began. It was a large sandstone complex comprised of three connected warehouses. The Market building was used as a community hub on Saturdays and showcased the best the area had to offer from local farmers and artisans. The middle building was the Theater. It was open in the front, and the back half housed a large screen and stage for movies, concerts, and plays. My personal favorite was the Art Museum. I enjoyed looking at the array of talent that enriched our small-town lives. Paintings, pottery, quilting, and jewelry were just a few of the items on display. I also reveled in the historical pieces that gave the public a glossed-over glimpse into the community's origins. A majority of the town turned out for this festival, so all three warehouses would be opened to accommodate the residents of Havenwood Falls.

After everyone was fed, the schedule then listed games and socializing in the square, followed by a parade of wagons leading up to the ball held in Mills Mansion.

Dad and I were in the Market area of the Annex, while Mom helped set up in the Art Building.

"Dad, when did you learn what your unique dragon gift was?" I handed him a chair.

"Well." He sat the chair down and turned to face me. "If I remember correctly, it was on my sixteenth birthday. That's roughly when it happens. Have you not discovered yours?"

I shook my head. "I keep thinking I'll wake up with some amazing revelation or ability. So far, nothing." Odd that I found that fact disappointing, considering it terrified me days ago.

"Don't worry. It'll happen when you need it to." He began to unfold another table.

"What does that mean?" I pouted a bit.

"It means that when you need that specific ability the most, it will surprise you." He continued to work.

"And that'll happen today?" I wasn't sure what to think of that piece of news.

"More than likely, sweetheart." He eyed some townsfolk approaching to help with tables and nodded in their direction.

I looked over and waved, then turned back to him. "I guess we'll have to finish this conversation later."

*Why do we always seem to get interrupted just when the conversation is getting good?*

"Absolutely." He winked at me.

I continued to set up chairs until every empty spot at the tables had a seat. I kept my mind on more pleasant things, like Jordan. I'd relived that kiss in the gazebo a hundred times since it happened. It was more thrilling than shifting and magical necklaces. It felt much like flying. Every time I thought of it, a tingle ran all the way down to my toes. As for Kai, I did my best not to think of him. His memory brought emotional chaos and confusion.

I looked forward to seeing Jordan at the dinner and ball. He was handsome in everyday clothing, and I could only imagine how fantastic he'd look in a suit. I was lingering on that mental picture when Miranda's voice interrupted my daydream.

"Zoey! I'm so excited!" She grabbed my arm and squeezed.

"Hey, what's up?" I tried not to let it show that she'd almost scared me witless.

"Guess who asked me to save a dance or two for him at the ball?" Her voice squeaked out a high-pitched sound.

I looked at her for a moment as I tried to figure out who could possibly make her this wound up. "Mr. Zander?"

She screwed up her face in disgust. "Ew, no. That'd be icky. He's old enough to be your dad."

"My dad? Why not your dad?"

"My dad is *really* old. Like, great-great-grandpa old, if I understand my mother correctly." She stuck her hands in her pockets.

"Oh yeah. I forgot about the immortality thing. My dad's older than you'd guess too, but not that old." I sighed. "Wait, I thought you had a thing for Mr. Zander?"

"Oh, he's nice to look at, but realistically that's about it. I need someone my own age . . . who won't go to jail for dating me." She giggled, and I had to join her. It was kind of absurd, once I gave it some consideration.

"Okay, so who is it then?" I couldn't think of anyone she'd shown specific interest in.

"Kai Reynolds." She beamed.

My eyebrows raised so high, I feared they'd disappear into my hairline. "Kai? The Kai that threatened me?" My brain screamed, *The Kai I've dreamed about?* No way I would admit that one out loud.

"Yes, same one." She sat on one of the chairs I'd just set up. "He's not all that bad when you get to know him. I've always thought he was cute. Besides, keep your friends close and your enemies closer." Her smile held a hint of mischief.

"Wait . . . what are you planning?" I sat next to her. "You don't really like him, do you?"

"I do, but I don't trust him. I'm not above using him to keep tabs on him." She waved a hand in front of me. "I know. I know. It's not the moral thing to do, but I think he's up to something. I don't want him ruining your big night. So, after a generous amount of flirting with him, he asked me to dance with him at the ball." She rubbed her hands together for maximum effect. "He will fall prey to my charms and drop all his devious plans."

"I'm not doubting your charms, Miranda, but what if it doesn't work?" I hoped she didn't take insult at my question.

She shrugged. "Then we'll have my cousins drag him off and keep him occupied."

I laughed out loud at that. "Oh, Miranda. You're such a joy in my life."

She sighed dramatically. "I'm glad someone appreciates me."

I grabbed her hand and gave it a squeeze. "Oh, you have no idea. I don't know what I'd do without you."

I looked in the mirror and fidgeted.

"Honey, you look beautiful. Stop fretting." Mom kissed the top of my head.

"I just don't want to embarrass myself." I turned my face to see if my hair was all still in place. Mom had curled it and piled it on top of my head, leaving a few ringlets to frame my face. Crystal-tipped bobby pins held it all in place, making my hair shine like the inside of our cave. I had to admit that my raven hair, with the unusual pearl-like streaks, looked fantastic all curled up.

"You won't embarrass yourself. You will be brilliant. Jordan will take one look at you and be knocked off his feet." She adjusted the bodice of my gown a little.

I tried not to blush. "You think?"

"No, I know. Now, time for the finishing touch." She slipped my grandmother's opal necklace around my neck.

The pendant felt cool against my bare skin. It matched very well with the light blue strapless gown I wore. The taffeta had a similar ability to shift colors with the lighting. I felt like Cinderella going to the ball. I only prayed it didn't end with me running away like a coward and leaving a trail of clothing behind me.

Mom adjusted her own dress, then placed a hand on my arm. "Ready?"

I nodded, we grabbed our coats, and I followed her outside to wait for Dad. We didn't have to wait long. He pulled the car up front, and we carefully seated ourselves. I did my best to keep the seatbelt from crushing my bodice.

In a few minutes, we were at the Annex and finding our seats at the table. Jordan had not yet arrived when we took our place, so I saved him a spot next to me.

The servers began to tend to each table. Plates were piled high with turkey, potatoes, beans, salads, and what looked like every dessert imaginable. I wasn't sure I'd ever seen that much food in my life. At first, I worried that this was an extravagant waste when there were so many in need, then I noticed something I wasn't expecting. People from all walks of life were present. Regardless of financial or social standing, everyone mingled together over a free meal and the joy of giving. It warmed my heart to see so much goodwill. Especially knowing that most of the time, various sects of the supernatural citizenry preferred to avoid each other.

I scanned the crowd, but didn't spot Jordan or his family. I wasn't totally sure his mom and dad would even attend, given their tense relationship. Then I saw them. Jordan's mom looked lovely in a pale yellow dress. Her makeup was impeccable, and her bruises were well hidden. It made me mad that she had injuries to hide in the first place, but at least she could attend and enjoy herself. Jordan stood close by, talking with . . . Katy.

My heart dropped to my stomach. She was cute, I couldn't deny that. She had more friends than I did as well. But surely Jordan wouldn't ditch me for her. He'd already committed to attending the celebration with me.

I saw Katy lean in and whisper something in his ear. He smiled and shook his head. As he turned to talk to his mother once more, Katy's gaze landed on me, and the satisfied smirk on her face caused me to see red. She obviously wanted to make me jealous. Sadly, it was working.

I turned my attention to my dad as we finished our meals. *It's okay*, I told myself. He'd find me soon.

As I picked at my dessert, I felt the hairs on the back of my neck stand to attention. I knew before I looked who I'd find standing behind me.

"Hello, Zoey." Kai's voice was deep and smooth, rubbing a balm over my wounded ego. I turned to see him standing with his hands in his trouser pockets. He wore a black tuxedo and looked like he'd stepped off the pages of GQ. I closed my mouth so I wouldn't openly gawk at his gorgeousness.

"Would you care to join me for a game of croquet? They have it set up across the street." He smiled down at me, and I had to remember to breathe.

I pulled my gaze from his and glanced around the tables once more. Jordan seemed to have disappeared. He could be in another part of the Annex, but why hadn't he sought me out yet?

"Sure, why not," I stammered as I stood. I moved to gather my plate, and he stopped me.

"They have people who will clean up afterwards." Kai took my hand and hooked it through his arm, then led me out the doors. We strolled in silence as we traversed a couple of blocks to the town square.

My fingers tingled where my skin touched the fabric of his jacket. I tried to ignore the sensations, but it was as if he sensed I wanted to pull away, so he hugged me closer to him as we walked.

"It's a lovely night. Almost as lovely as you," he murmured as we strolled across the grass.

I felt the heat rush to my cheeks. "Thank you, that's very kind."

"Nothing kind about it. I'm simply telling the truth." He passed the game of croquet that was already in progress.

"Wait? I thought we were going to play—"

He cut off my sentence with a finger to my lips. "Shh . . . let's just enjoy each other's company for a while."

My senses heightened. Something felt wrong. Something had been off from the moment he first spoke to me. I just couldn't place it. The attraction I felt still lingered, but it was engulfed in a veil of danger. My instincts urged me to get away from him.

"Kai, I should get back. I need to speak with my parents before the parade begins." I backed away.

He followed me, a grin pulling up the corners of his lips and exposing the tip of his fangs. "What's your hurry, sweet Zoey? We haven't had a chance to really get acquainted yet."

I shook my head. "You don't want to know me. I don't know what you want, but it isn't me."

He took one more step, and as I moved to avoid him, my back hit a solid object. I looked around to find myself up against a large tree, inconveniently hiding us from the view of many in the square.

Kai put his arms on either side of me. "Oh, but it is you I'm interested in. You're special, Zoey. And those of us who are special should stick together." He leaned in close, and his gaze captured mine. I felt locked in that stare. My limbs refused to move. He put one hand behind my neck and pulled me close to him, then pressed his lips to mine. For a moment I relaxed, reliving the dream I'd had, then my mind screamed at me to run. This felt too familiar. We'd done this before, yet I knew we hadn't. *That dream! He did something to cause that dream!* I pushed at his chest, but he barely moved. My next instinct was to bring my knee up as hard as I could. He froze, then backed away, squatting a little as he stumbled backward.

I turned and ran.

~

THE FEW GAMES that had been set up on the square were scarcely occupied. Not too many people were willing to brave the colder air outside of the Annex, but there were a few who donned their coats and took part in the fun.

I ran toward them, praying Kai wasn't following me. I stopped near a bean bag game to catch my breath when a stray bag flew right into me, knocking me off balance and into the person next to me, who then spilled his punch all over my dress. I froze in place, surveying the damage to my skirt. My beautiful blue taffeta had been drenched with pink splotches.

I closed my eyes. "I will not cry. I will not cry," I whispered to myself over and over. When I opened my eyes, Katy and her two minions stood in front of me.

"Oops. I'm so clumsy. I'm so very sorry, Zoey. I ruined your dress, and the ball hasn't even started yet." Katy pouted as she spoke loudly, assuring bystanders heard her apology. "Here, let me help you get cleaned up."

She grabbed my arm, and her friends gathered behind me and gave me a not-so-gentle push. They rushed me over toward the Annex, but once we were out of sight, they shoved me over to the gazebo.

"I warned you, freak." Katy glared at me. "You have no business here or with Jordan. And now you're cozying up to Kai, too? What a hussy."

I stepped back from them and touched my opal, letting its soothing influence rush over me. "You do realize that my grandfather runs this shindig we're attending tonight? That my family is one of the founding families of Havenwood Falls?" I put my hands on my hips. "If anyone doesn't belong, I'm guessing it's you. And you hate that. Kai and Jordan are both interested in me, and you hate that, too. You're a jealous hag."

Katy bristled. "Oh, you think you're so high and mighty because you have the Mills name? But your family are a bunch of thieving, back-stabbing freaks, and you should all be run out of town."

"What?" I asked. "What the hell are you babbling on about?"

She stepped closer to me and pointed a finger in my face. "Your grandfather and his crappy investment advice cost my family everything. We lost our vacation home, our nicest cars . . . everything that was important to me."

"Oh lord. That's what all this is about?" I rolled my eyes. "You need to get a grip, Katy. You obviously don't know how investing works. Nothing is ever a sure thing. Haven't you paid attention in economics?" I sighed. "I don't know what advice your family did or did not take from my grandfather, but I'm hardly responsible for that."

An angry sound formed in her throat, and for a moment, I thought she would attack me.

"Have you paid attention tonight? Did you notice Jordan has avoided you the entire evening?" She smiled sweetly, but it was full of venom. "I told him all about you. He wants nothing to do with someone like you."

"And just what did you tell him?" I waited.

She glanced at her manicure, as if the conversation bored her. "I told him how you use people to get what you want, then discard them. I told him that you thought he was beneath you because his family isn't in your social circles. Do you know what he said?" She batted her eyes innocently. "He said he'd only asked you out because he felt sorry for you. The new girl in town that no one liked. He's such a nice guy that he wanted to help." She fanned herself dramatically. "He's a keeper for sure. Too bad it won't be you he chooses when it's all said and done."

My blood boiled. *It couldn't be true, could it?*

"I think that's quite enough, Katy." Aunt Jetta stood just behind me. Then I saw Miranda step up next to her.

"Oh good. Another Mills freak. Why do you all look like you belong on *The Addams Family?*" Katy sneered.

Aunt Jetta stepped around me. "You haven't begun to see freak, sweetheart."

Katy opened her mouth, but snapped it closed again. Her confused expression told me she hadn't expected an admission of our freakishness. It took some of the sting from her barbs.

Miranda walked up to Katy, almost nose to nose, and stared into her eyes. "You know, Katy, you keep using the word freak, but if you really knew the truth, you and your greasy gremlins there would crap . . . your . . . pants."

Katy stepped back, her eyes as wide as saucers. I placed my hand on Miranda's arm.

"She's not worth our time. Come help me clean my dress. We have a ball to attend."

We all three turned to walk away, but Katy managed to muster one last burst of courage, and she grabbed my arm.

"Don't you turn your back on me when I'm speaking to you, freak!" The rage in her voice mingled with desperation. She had lost her power over me, and she knew it.

I pulled her close to me, my dragon granting me a strength in my grip that Katy couldn't escape from. My voice came out low and had a slight growl that mingled with the syllables. "If you ever touch me, or any of my friends again, I will not only end you, but I'll end your entire family."

I felt my eyes flash, and my vision blurred for mere seconds before returning to normal. I'd give her a glimpse of what she was dealing with. Not enough to get me in trouble, but enough to make her wonder what she truly saw.

I released her wrist, and she backed away quickly, blindly groping at her friends' jackets as she pulled them with her. She didn't utter another word as they all three turned and scampered away.

# CHAPTER 10

"Worst birthday ever," I complained as we stood in the bathroom of the Annex and rubbed my skirt with a wet paper towel.

Aunt Jetta kissed my forehead. "It's been eventful, but I promise you that my sixteenth was much worse. Remind me to tell you about it sometime."

"It's not over yet. You may find yourself defending that title before the night is up." I groaned. "Is this coming out?"

Miranda moved her face closer to the material. "Probably as good as it's gonna get."

I tossed the towel in the trash and dried my hands.

"You know," Miranda said, "for a few moments there, I understood why my kind eat people."

Aunt Jetta laughed. "Yeah, it's tempting sometimes, isn't it?"

I looked up. "Did dragons ever eat people? I know the fairy tales always make us out to be man-eaters."

"Some did, but I think that's more the style of the fire-breathing kind. As a general rule, frost dragons didn't. We preferred to live in peace." She looked in the mirror and adjusted some strands of her hair that the wind had misplaced. "We've pretty much always been more about fish, seals, etc. The old country was full of that stuff." She applied a fresh coat of lipstick. "That doesn't mean that frost dragons haven't ever eaten someone, though. It's totally possible." She smirked.

"No, thanks." I said. "Katy's so spoiled, she'd taste bad."

Miranda laughed. "No doubt."

Aunt Jetta exited the bathroom and held the door open for us. We left the building and rushed back to the area near the square where everyone stood waiting for the parade to start.

"Are we really gonna ride in those all the way to Grandpa's?" I asked, pointing to the row of wagons pulling into place.

"Sure are," Aunt Jetta said.

Miranda grabbed my hand. "Come on. Let's grab a seat on the outside. I hate riding in the middle."

As we neared the horse-drawn wagons, I noticed that each one had built-in bench seats and could hold quite a few people. Miranda and I were helped up, and we settled into seats near the front. Aunt Jetta waved to us as she climbed into a nearby wagon to sit with a friend of hers.

"Do you really think Jordan is just taking pity on me?" I didn't mean to blurt out the question at that moment, but it had been bothering me.

"I don't." Miranda placed her hand over one of mine. "I've never known him to be that heartless. Kind? Yes. Shallow? No."

"So why do you think he's avoided me all night? I haven't even gotten so much as a hello." My heart broke at the thought.

"I'm not sure, but my guess is he isn't intentionally ignoring you." She glanced around the square.

I shrugged. "I hope you're right."

She gave my hand another squeeze, and in that moment, the horses began to pull us out of town and up toward Havenwood Heights.

People chatted all around us as I took in the scenery before me. It was lovely. Businesses were lit up for the celebration. Various celestial ornamentation mingled with Christmas decorations. Once we reached the residential areas, the lights changed to solely those of the

Christmas variety. The soothing clop of the horse's hooves, the snow, and the lights all gave me the illusion of serenity. It didn't last long, but I treasured what I could get.

We pulled up in front of Grandpa's house, and my eyes immediately went to the stone dragons. Grandpa Mills stood at the top of the stairs, watching the wagons arrive. Once everyone had unloaded, he picked up a bullhorn to speak. I had to stifle a giggle, knowing he could growl loud enough to shake the ground beneath us all.

"Welcome to my home, everyone! Please enter and let us dance and give thanks to the gods for the protection of our lovely little town." He lowered the bullhorn and handed it off to a man standing nearby. Then he hobbled inside, and people began to follow. A lady took our coats as we passed through the entryway.

Soon we were standing in a large ballroom at the back of the house. Once again, my breath caught, as I was taken aback by the beauty of the room. There were crystal candelabras everywhere, each one of them holding six lit candles. A large skylight graced the ceiling and allowed a perfect view of the moon. The only artificial light present came from two small chandeliers at each end of the room.

One wall had been lined with tables loaded down with drinks and appetizers. Each table had a large vase of fresh cut flowers.

I leaned into Miranda. "Where does he get fresh flowers this time of year?" I asked.

"I'm told he flies them in from all over the country." She seemed unimpressed by that detail.

The music started, and I turned to face her. "Weren't you planning on charming the grouch out of Kai?"

I debated telling her about my encounter with him earlier. Maybe if she kept him busy, he'd leave me alone. I knew she could handle herself if he stepped out of line.

"Oh yeah, I guess I should find him. Will you be okay?" She looked concerned.

"Yeah, I'll be fine. If I need reinforcements, I'll let you know. Just . . . don't take any crap from him." I gave her a smile and a light shove toward the dance floor. She turned to wink at me and then began her search for Kai.

I stood to one side and swayed with the music while others spun around on the floor.

"Would you like to dance, birthday girl?" I looked up to see my father, hand stretched out for mine.

I nodded. "That'd be nice."

He led me to the middle of the floor, and we began a country dance that I recognized from gym class. We'd been taught several dances especially for the ball.

"I'm sorry we haven't done anything big for your birthday. This celebration has kept us all busy. I promise to make it up to you." He spun me around and then back to him.

"It's okay, Dad. I know it's been crazy." I stepped back two steps, then forward two steps.

"It's your sweet sixteen, but I have a feeling it hasn't been so sweet."

I shrugged. "It could have been worse."

Dad stopped and turned around. I saw Jordan standing behind him. "Mind if I cut in?" he asked my dad.

Dad smiled. "Sure thing." He bowed to me before he walked away.

Jordan grasped my hand in his and placed his other at my waist. "How are you liking the festivities so far?"

"How am I liking it?" I couldn't believe he'd asked me that. "Well, outside of having punch spilled on my dress, being bullied by three jerks, accosted by . . . never mind who it was, and my date ditching me all through dinner, it's been peachy." I couldn't keep the sarcasm from my voice.

He stopped. "I'm sorry, Zoey. I didn't mean to abandon you. It's just . . . something happened, and I couldn't get to you until now."

I pulled my hand from his. "Yeah. No problem."

I walked away from him and toward the double doors that led to the backyard. Without stopping, I pushed through them, letting them swing shut behind me. I glanced around and remembered Grandpa had a huge garden to the right, so I walked the path until I was surrounded by evergreens and hedges. That's when I heard the commotion.

"Dad, you've gotta stop this. You're being ridiculous." My dad's voice echoed loud and clear.

"Don't tell me what I have to do, boy. This is my home." He shouted, but not like he had the night we had dinner with him. It sounded human.

"Daddy, I'm a grown woman. I can wear what I want." Aunt Jetta's voice was completely devoid of emotion.

I silently made my way to the edge of one of the larger hedges and peeked around it.

Grandpa pointed to my aunt's leather dress. "That is not a gown. It looks like something out of some smutty catalog. And your tattoos are completely visible."

"My dress is completely appropriate for this occasion. It covers all my naughty bits." She smiled as his face turned red at the mention of her naughty bits. "And my tattoos are part of me. They go where I go."

"It's a fine day when my own daughter has less respect for me than my human daughter-in-law," he grumbled.

"Well, see? You've been wrong about her all this time," Aunt Jetta said. "She's actually an amazing person, but you won't take your blinders off to see it."

"She's human!" Grandpa Mills growled.

"She's my wife." Dad's tone held a warning.

Grandpa turned to Dad. "And now your own daughter is chasing after a human boy. This is your fault, Tristan." He pointed a bony finger at my dad.

I'd heard enough, and I stepped out. "What is wrong with you people?" I shouted. "Why can't you get along for more than five minutes?"

Suddenly, Kai and Miranda came pushing through the hedges behind me. Kai looked at me, then Grandpa. "I'm sorry, sir. I tried."

Miranda hauled off and punched Kai in the gut. He doubled over. "That's for conspiring against my best friend, you jerk."

My heart broke. "Grandpa? *You* were trying to keep me from Jordan?"

He had the decency to look guilty. "Honey, he's human. It'll never work. I forbid it!"

Tears filled my eyes. "It's been a horrible day already, but to find out that my own flesh and blood worked out a plan to break my heart is more than I can bear. And on my birthday, too."

My vision blurred. I turned and ran back the way I came, running straight into Jordan. *Great. Can my luck get any worse?*

# CHAPTER 11

*I* swiped at the tears on my cheeks as Jordan stood in front of me.

"Zoey, let me explain. Please." He held his hands out to me.

I stepped back, not wanting him to touch me. "Fine. Explain."

I crossed my arms and waited for him to say something—anything—that would make me feel better. At the same time, I wasn't sure if I could trust him. He did ignore me most of the night. I tried to push Katy's awful words from my mind.

"My mom came tonight. She hasn't in recent years, but it was nice to see her enjoy the celebration for once." He smiled for a brief moment. "Then Kai told me he needed to speak with me. The next thing I knew, he'd locked me in a closet in the Annex. It took almost an hour before someone heard me yelling and let me out."

I frowned. "I'm so sorry, Jordan. Kai is a deceitful jerk, thanks to a directive from my grandpa."

"Your grandpa? Why would he do that?" He looked as confused as I expected him to be.

"It's hard to explain." I couldn't very well tell him the truth.

"Okay." He paused. "Well, when I finally found my mom, Dad had shoved her into the car. He was drunk and yelling at her. Accusing her of flirting with all the men around her." He shook his head.

95

"Nothing was further from the truth. He's just so jealous, he can't see straight, especially when he's had too much to drink."

"Oh no. Is she okay?" I worried she'd been beat up again.

"Yeah, she's fine. My father, on the other hand . . ." He sighed. "I managed to get her away from him, and a friend of hers is looking after her. I punched my dad, and his head hit the trunk. It knocked him out cold. He's currently sleeping it off in the car."

"You're wrong about that, son." An angry voice spoke from the shadows, then the man I assumed to be his dad stepped forward. He looked at me. "Is this the little hussy you've been lusting after? They're all the same, son. They aren't worth your time."

"You don't know what you're talking about. Zoey is a lady. Mom is a wonderful woman. If you were sober for more than five minutes a day, you'd know that."

Mr. Woods stepped forward and raised his hand.

"No!" I yelled and instinctively stepped in front of Jordan.

Mr. Woods stopped and looked at me. "Stay out of this, or you'll get what's coming to you, too."

Jordan pulled me to his side. "You won't touch her."

Mr. Woods shook his head and chuckled. "She must be something in the sack to make you stand up to me."

Jordan threw a punch. "Do not talk about Zoey like that. She's the most honest, loving, and kind person I know. She deserves respect, and you will give it to her." His voice held years of pent-up anger.

"Ha! I don't think so, boy." Mr. Woods rubbed the spot where Jordan had hit him. "Ain't a female in this world deserves respect from a man."

He lunged forward and tackled Jordan, knocking me to the ground, as well. I hit with a hard thud and felt something pop in my ankle. I cried out in pain.

My grandfather's loud and menacing voice broke through the chaos. "Thomas Woods. You take your hands off that boy right now."

Mr. Woods sat on the ground, straddling Jordan, smacking him in the face. "This is my son, old man. I'll discipline him however I please."

"No, you won't." The sound of my own voice startled me. It was me, yet it wasn't quite me. I could hear the subtle growl of my dragon filtering through.

Mr. Woods took a step back.

Grandpa pushed forward and glared at Mr. Woods, then looked at me. "Do you see how they behave? This is what you want to shackle yourself to?"

Kai spoke up then. "Despite my orders from your grandfather, I'm still very interested in you, Zoey. I'd be honored to save you from yourself."

Enough was enough. The anger and frustration I'd buried pushed to the surface, and instead of tamping it down, I gave it free rein.

"I am not a toy to play with! Nor am I a servant to be bossed around. I will make my own decisions, and none of you will tell me how to live my life." I hobbled forward, my ankle causing me to wince in pain. "You!" I pointed at my grandfather. "How dare you decide what's best for me. You ignored me for over fifteen years. You have no right to expect a say in my future now." I shook my head. "Manipulating my feelings for your own ridiculous prejudices is beyond despicable. You are a mean, selfish old man. What other miseries have you inflicted in my life?"

Grandpa growled. "I do what I must for this family."

"Oh really? Like exiling your own son because he fell in love with an amazing woman? Ignoring your grandchild? Torturing your daughter because she lives life to the fullest? That's how you help them?" I scoffed. "I'd hate to see what you'd do if you didn't care."

Jetta stepped forward and gave me a slow clap, the look on her face full of appreciation.

I turned to Kai. "You had the gall to not only pretend to like me, but I'm pretty sure you used some of your . . . gifts," I spoke the word as if it caused a bad taste in my mouth, "to manipulate my feelings for you. Dreams? Really? That's low. I have zero attraction to you now, and I'm quite sure I never did." I leaned closer, putting my weight on my good ankle. "Oh, and if you ever put your hands on me again, I'll make sure you sing soprano for weeks."

Jetta snorted as she held back her gleeful laughter. I knew she enjoyed watching me dole out the tongue-lashings that were long overdue.

I turned to Jordan. "I like you, Jordan, but there are a lot of things you don't know about me. Things you'll have to accept if you want to be a part of my life."

He nodded. "I can handle that."

I shook my head and fought back the sadness that began to overtake me. "I'm not sure you can."

Mr. Woods stepped forward. "See? She's worthless, son. Walk away while you still can."

Jordan's rage flared again, and he swung at his dad, this time missing. His father threw a punch and knocked Jordan to the ground, blood oozing from his lip.

I stepped forward, this time ignoring the pain, and grabbed Mr. Woods' jacket. "Don't you ever hit him or your wife again."

He gasped, and it was then that I realized I'd lifted him high enough off the ground that his feet were dangling.

I put him back on solid ground, then shoved him away. He staggered, then lunged at me. My father and Aunt Jetta grabbed him on either side before he reached his intended target.

"Jordan, what would you like us to do?" my father asked.

Jordan blinked. "Do?"

Aunt Jetta nodded. "We can put him in jail."

Dad's grip on Mr. Woods' arm tightened, and the man winced. "Or . . . we could banish him."

Aunt Jetta smiled. "That would work."

Grandpa muttered something under his breath.

"Banish?" Jordan looked completely confused.

"We can send him away. He'll live out his life peacefully, if he so chooses, and never bother you or your mother again," Dad answered.

Jetta released Mr. Woods and pulled Jordan aside. She whispered to him, out of earshot of his father. I assumed she was giving him further details on the exile they suggested.

After a couple of minutes, my nerves were stretched thin. My ankle hurt, and all I wanted to do was get away from everyone. I hobbled to the line of trees behind Grandpa's house.

"I need to be alone," I shouted as I slowly walked away. "Don't bother looking for me."

"Zoey, can I come with you?" Jordan asked.

I froze. *Do I want his company?* I wasn't sure. Tears rolled down my cheeks, and I swiped at them, trying to hide the evidence of my heartache.

"If you like," I murmured, unsure if he could even hear me. I limped forward into the forest until I reached a large log. The pain became intense, and I knew I couldn't make it where I wanted to go. The cave.

I sat down, and tears fell once more. I brushed them away before I pushed my skirt aside and rubbed my sore ankle. Jordan walked only a few feet behind me. He'd been following in silence, allowing me my privacy until I was ready to address him.

As I continued to rub my ankle, the pain began to subside. I had no idea what had happened, but it felt as if it were healing. I was astonished at what appeared to be happening before my eyes.

"Can I sit?" asked Jordan.

I blinked up at him, trying to clear my head. "Sure."

He scooted close to me and reached for my hand. "I don't know what's going on, but you can trust me, Zoey. I would never turn away from you."

I chuckled with self-deprecation. "You say that now."

"No, I mean it. There is nothing that you could say or do that would scare me off." He gave my hand a squeeze.

I looked into his eyes, and the decision was made. I would tell him and let the chips fall where they may.

"Jordan? I'm a dragon."

# CHAPTER 12

*J*ordan laughed awkwardly. "Right."

"I'm not kidding." My expression was solemn.

"How is that possible? You look human to me." The timbre in his voice indicated he still thought I was joking.

"I'm a shifter. I'm half human and half dragon." I stood. "I can show you, if you like."

His eyes narrowed. "Um . . .okay." Obviously, he was still skeptical.

"Turn around," I ordered. "I have to undress before I change."

His eyebrows shot up. "Do I have to?" his tone teased.

I couldn't help but smile a little. "Yes, you have to. My dad is a dragon, too, and if he thinks you saw me naked, he might be tempted to eat you."

Jordan shrugged and turned his back to me, moving his legs to the other side of the log.

I reached back and unzipped my dress, letting it fall and pool at my feet. My shoes were next, along with my undergarments. I stepped back into the darkness and picked a somewhat open spot to transform.

"You promise you won't freak out?" I shouted from my hiding spot in the shadows.

"I promise," he yelled back.

I summoned my inner dragon and let her take over. Popping, cracking, stretching—sensations I was becoming accustomed to took over as I left the human Zoey behind.

I stepped forward as quietly as possible, then put my muzzle close to Jordan's back and snorted. Frost covered his back, and he shivered.

"Hey, no throwing snowballs while my back is—" He turned around and froze. "Oh, dear God." He scooted back off the log and landed on his butt in the frost-covered leaves.

I placed my head on the log and looked at him, hoping he could see that I meant him no harm.

"Zoey?" He stood and took a cautious step forward.

I gave a slight nod, then closed my eyes, not wanting to see the fear on his face that I knew would be present.

I felt a hand rub my nose. "Unbelievable," he whispered.

I opened my eyes, and Jordan smiled, awe and wonder filling his eyes. "Wow. I knew you were amazing, special. But this . . . I hadn't even scratched the surface."

I blinked, letting a tear fall. He leaned forward and placed his cheek up against me. "I care about you, Zoey. This doesn't change that."

I closed my eyes.

He reached out and touched the opal that miraculously still hung from my giant neck. "Please, come back to me. You're beautiful like this, but I'd like to talk."

I slowly raised my head and moved to look at where my clothes still lay.

Jordan noticed the pile of fabric. "Do you need me to turn around again?"

I nodded once more.

He turned his back and said, "Let me know when it's safe to look again. I don't want your dad eating me."

The human side of me chuckled, although I think through the dragon it came out as an odd growl.

I closed my eyes and summoned my human form. I felt myself

shrink and compress. In moments, I once again became sixteen-year-old Zoey Mills. I quickly grabbed my clothes and shimmied into them, leaving only my gown to be zipped.

"Okay, I'm dressed," I said as I walked up behind him.

Jordan turned to me and reached forward to cup my cheek. I was still terrified. *How could he be okay with this? At best, he can't possibly see a future for us as a couple.*

He leaned forward and kissed me lightly on the lips. "It's cold out here."

I nodded. "It is. You need your coat."

He glanced at me. "Do you need one? You don't seem to be cold at all."

I shrugged. "I'm not. Perks of being a frost dragon."

"Huh. That's cool," he said.

I looked at him. "Was that a pun?"

He chuckled. "Not a good one."

I laughed, too. "True."

He shivered again.

"Maybe we should get you back to the house," I suggested.

"I'm okay. I want to stay here with you." His teeth were starting to chatter.

"It's hard to talk if you die of hypothermia. Let's go back. I promise to stick around and talk."

He nodded and grew somber.

"Are you okay?" I asked.

"Yeah, just thinking about my dad." He sighed.

"I understand. Did my dad explain banishment?"

He nodded. "Sort of. I didn't understand it fully, but it sounds better than going through this hell over and over."

"What did you decide then?" I asked.

"I told him to do whatever it took to make it stop. If that meant erasing his memory, or whatever it was, I'm fine with that. My mom would be heartbroken, but she'd get over it. Her heart will heal faster than her bones." His mouth formed a grim line.

I put my hand in his as we walked back to my grandfather's house.

~

JORDAN, Aunt Jetta, Miranda, and I sat in front of the fire at my house. Dad had dropped us off at home, and Mom had made us all hot chocolate, so we sipped it as we talked.

Aunt Jetta happily filled Jordan in on the basics of our species, relishing all the unique attributes of being a dragon. He was captivated.

"Of course, we aren't supposed to share this secret with humans, unless we have valid justification. You can never tell anyone. Ever. Do you understand that, Jordan?" Aunt Jetta's eyes bored into his.

Jordan nodded. "Absolutely. I'll take it to the grave."

Aunt Jetta's lips turned up into a devious grin. "I have no doubt about that. I like you, kid, but if you spill this information to anyone you aren't supposed to, I'll eat you for breakfast."

Jordan's eyes widened. "I read you loud and clear."

"Smart guy," Jetta said as she patted him on the back.

"So how does the whole dragon relationship thing work?" he asked. "Do you look for someone just like you?" He paused. "I'm sorry. I don't know how to ask this without sounding stupid."

I understood. "You want to know how we choose a life partner?"

He nodded.

I reached up and caressed my necklace, amazed I still had it. It's like it changed with me when I shifted. "Well, I guess like everyone else. We find someone we like and if things work out, then there ya go." I suddenly felt much wiser than my sixteen years. *Thank you once again, dear dragon.*

Aunt Jetta held up her hands. "Don't look at me. I haven't found it yet."

Mom set down her mug and smiled. "Yes, that sums it up." She looked at Jordan point blank. "And Jordan, if you really like Zoey, there is nothing to stop you two from being together."

His eyes filled with emotion. I recognized it as hope. "Really?"

Mom nodded. "Absolutely. It worked out okay for me."

"Whoa," he said. "You're not a dragon, either?"

"Nope. I'm as human as you are."

He looked at me and reached for my hand. "I'm willing to try if you are, Zoey. I really do care about you."

I blushed a bit. "That'd be nice."

My dad walked into the room and ruined the moment. Jordan dropped my hand. Dad's expression was grim. "Heidi Bennet was seen fighting with her boyfriend at the ball. She ran into the woods and hasn't been seen since. They're organizing a search party. I told them to call me when they were ready to head out."

Mom and Aunt Jetta exchanged worried glances. A human in the woods at night is never a good combination, especially in Havenwood Falls.

"Jordan." Dad sat down in a chair across from us. "Can I speak with you a moment? It's about your dad."

Jordan went pale. I took his hand in mine once more as a show of support. Jordan swallowed and nodded.

Dad cleared his throat. "Your dad is fine. I flew him to a wooded area just outside of Grand Junction. Then gave him explicit instructions to forget about his family and Havenwood Falls."

Jordan frowned. "Does he know?"

Dad nodded. "He does now."

"But, won't he tell everyone?" Jordan asked.

Dad grinned. "Who's gonna believe a guy that's slobbering drunk?"

"What about when he's sober?" Jordan asked.

"Not a problem, either. As I told you before, this town has a special ward on it. Once you leave Havenwood Falls, you only have a certain number of days to return or you forget you were ever here. Your dad won't remember his life here. And it's not likely he'll ever stumble back in. This town has a way of keeping itself hidden."

Jordan bit his lower lip, and I assumed it was all sinking in.

"He'll never harm you or your mother again. And as for employment, I've already offered your mom a job at the pawn shop. It's not the best pay, but it'll help until we find her something she likes better."

Jordan's eyes filled with tears of appreciation. "Thank you so much, Mr. Mills. I can't begin to explain the service you've done us."

"No need to thank us." He smiled and leaned forward to give Jordan's hand a firm shake.

I looked at my dad. "What about Grandpa?"

He scratched his head. "He's a stubborn old man who's stuck in his ways. He's angry and will still be someone we must contend with. We'll just have to keep working on him."

I frowned.

"Don't let him bother you, Zoey. You gave him some real food for thought tonight. I imagine he'll be stewing on that for a while."

"Sounds promising," I said.

"Oh," said Dad. "Are you okay? I noticed you were in pain earlier, after Mr. Woods pushed you."

I lifted my leg and pulled my skirt up to expose my ankle. "It was weird. I sprained my ankle pretty bad when I landed. When I got to the woods and sat down, I rubbed my ankle, and it started to feel a bit better."

Dad and Aunt Jetta exchanged glances.

"What? What does that mean?" I asked.

Aunt Jetta leaned toward me. "Were you crying by any chance?"

I thought about it. "Yeah, I was. But only a little."

"Did you happen to get tears on your ankle?"

"Maybe from my hands?"

Aunt Jetta smiled. "That's your unique gift, Zoey. Your tears have healing properties."

"That's a wonderful gift, but keep it a secret," Mom said. "Other supernaturals would kill to get their hands on your tears."

Dad's face was somber.

"Why?" I asked in alarm.

"There are several things about dragons that have magical properties. For some, it's their scales, others their blood, and most rarely, their tears . . . and these are just some of the reasons a dragon would be killed and harvested. I'm not trying to scare you, just inform you of the dangers of not being discreet." He looked pointedly at Jordan. "Her life could be at risk if you were to leak this to anyone. Do you understand that?"

Jordan nodded. "Yes, sir. I would never put her in harm's way."

"Glad to hear it. Now, let's get out that birthday cake we never ate. How does that sound?" Dad rubbed his hands together in glee. He loved cake.

Mom brought in the cake and I blew out the candles. They sang Happy Birthday to me, and for the first time in years, I felt I belonged. I felt strong and capable. I could withstand anything life threw my way. I could stand up for myself and be proud of who I was.

My awesome aunt, my amazing parents, my best friend, and possibly the love of my life were there by my side. What more could I ask for? Best. Birthday. Ever.

~

WE HOPE you enjoyed this story in the Havenwood Falls High series of novellas featuring a variety of supernatural creatures. Read on for an excerpt of *Awaken the Soul* (A Havenwood Falls High Novella) by Michele G. Miller. The series is a collaborative effort by multiple authors. Each book is generally a stand-alone, so you can read them in any order, although some authors will be writing sequels to their own stories. Please be aware when you choose your next read.

HAVENWOOD FALLS BOOKS by Amy Hale:

*Somewhere Within*
*Blood & Iron*
*Flames Among the Frost*
*Betrayal Among the Frost*

OTHER BOOKS you might enjoy in the Young Adult Havenwood Falls High series:

*Written in the Stars* by Kallie Ross

*Bound by Shadows* by Cameo Renae
*Saving Infiniti* by Rose Garcia
*Predestined* by Valia Lind

Stay up to date at www.HavenwoodFalls.com

# ABOUT THE AUTHOR

Since childhood, Amy Hale has been creating exceptional stories that summon a whirlwind of emotions and inspiration unto the reader. She loves creating characters and worlds from nothing but her imagination and a few glasses of wine. Her love of the written word has not only resulted in her writing some of her readers' favorite adventures, but has also manifested itself in the form of book hoarding. She's convinced it's not a sickness.

She debuted her first fiction novel in 2015, after retiring from thirteen years of non-fiction writing for various online entities. For the last couple of decades, she's also carried the titles of Laundry Goddess, Chef, Butt Wiper, Soother of Temper Tantrums, and in more recent years, Moderator of Sarcastic Eyerolls and Sass. She resides in Illinois with her husband, as well as two grown children who claim they are never moving out. Regardless, they are the center of her universe, although her cat believes otherwise.

If she had any spare time, she'd love music, photography, watching Mystery Science Theater 3000 with her family, and long rides on the back of her husband's motorcycle.

Learn more at authoramyhale.com.

# ACKNOWLEDGMENTS

I first must give thanks to God for this amazing path He has put me on. I am nothing without Him.

I owe an unfathomable debt to my husband John. He has been patient with me as I chase this amazing dream. He has given me strength when I felt like giving up. He has showered love on me when I was at my worst. I am blessed to have you by my side, dear husband. I love you!

I'm thrilled to be a part of the Havenwood Falls family. Many thanks to Kristie Cook for inviting me to join this amazing and talented group. I also appreciate the help and guidance you've given me through this project, Kristie. Love ya, dear friend!

I want to send some huge thanks my Havenwood Falls sisters E.J. Fechenda, for the use of Willow, and Michele G. Miller, for letting me borrow the Annex. They were perfect additions to my story!

Mad love for Regina Wamba for giving my cover the perfect look. I couldn't have envisioned anything better!

I owe a million hugs to my friend and partner in crime Terri Wilson. Thank you for keeping me calm and organized when I felt anything but.

To my Havenwood Falls family, which grows every day, thank you for being so supportive of me. Your enthusiasm, brainstorming sessions, and loving encouragement have meant the world to me. I'm excited to see us all build this amazing world together.

Thank you to the readers, who have kept me striving for excellence. Your reviews and comments have helped me improve and grow my craft. Thank you for spending time with me and my characters.

HAVENWOOD FALLS HIGH

Awaken the Soul

MICHELE G. MILLER

~ A Havenwood Falls Young Adult Novella ~

## *Awaken the Soul* (A Havenwood Falls High Novella) by Michele G. Miller

Breckin Roberts has known Vivienne his entire life. Born and raised in Havenwood Falls, they attend the same school, eat at the same restaurants, and enjoy the same festivals. But they aren't friends. They're merely two classmates—her human and him not so much. Until one fateful December afternoon.

When Vivienne Freeman awakens late that night, disheveled and disoriented, the last thing she remembers is going for a run, but something feels . . . off. It's not until the gorgeous but ever elusive Breckin Roberts approaches her out of the blue that she learns she almost died. And he's the one who saved her.

Or so he thought.

Turns out, saving Vivienne has opened her to a whole new kind of danger. Breckin is an angel who interfered with Death. It's a slight easily forgiven, if not for the connection he awakens while healing her. A connection one reaper finds highly appealing. A connection that could turn Vivienne into a pawn in the battle of good versus evil—a battle about to descend on Havenwood Falls.

# AWAKEN THE SOUL

## AN EXCERPT

White.

Everywhere I look. Pure, undiluted, untouched.

Colorado in December.

Banking left, the tip of my wing disturbs a snow-laden pine bough, scattering ice crystals. The mountain forest is peaceful this late in the afternoon, though the threat of a storm lurks in the gray sky. A gust rolls in from the north, and I snap my wings, letting the airstream guide my path toward home.

*How long will this peace last?* This morning's message from Elias served as an eerie reminder of my time limit. Four months. Tucking my wings, I shift, free-falling toward the ground, dodging trees as I dart in and around the woods. Freedom. I arch skyward, shooting high above Mount Alexa. The ground, the falls, the trees—they are blemishes on a snowy white canvas.

A scream penetrates the peace. I twist, levitating among the clouds, my gaze narrowing on the ground far below.

The crimson trail, smeared for yards before the dense forest covers the evidence, is hard to miss.

Blood. Thick, human blood.

This is Havenwood Falls—it's not an abnormal occurrence in the forest. But . . .

I dive, lured by a scent that burns my nostrils and confuses my senses.

I'm on the ground within moments of her scream. Her keening death cries prick at my skin, sending an unfamiliar sensation skittering up my spine and across my wings. Angry snarls join her moans. I should leave, yet I press on—following the blood trail. The creature drags her instead of making a clean kill. Most shifters kill, rather than play with, their food. I maintain distance, preferring to remain in the good graces of the other supernatural beings within Havenwood Falls. Angel or not, minding my business keeps the peace. History has proven this. The world is a better place when all creatures, good and evil, play nice together. That type of thinking will be my downfall in four months, if I'm not careful.

An unnatural calm claims the still woods, and my senses sharpen. I move forward as an ache builds up in my chest. Her cries diminish, but her scent strengthens. It's familiar. The spicy combination of ginger root and mint. I duck beneath low branches and break through thicker brush, my steps quickening as I track them. Another growl disturbs the woods, and I pause. Twenty feet ahead, a shadow of fur and menace crosses my path—retreating. The feeling in my chest intensifies like a fist crushing my heart.

Ginger, mint, and something—more. They inundate me as I maneuver around a thick tree and come to a stop.

She is bathed in blood. Her long golden hair spreads around her head, a silken halo on a snowy pillow of white. From my vantage point, I cannot see her face, but her scent—her perfume—gives her away.

*Vivienne Freeman.*

And above her lifeless body, he is ageless and brings with him the kiss of death. A reaper. His corporeal existence remains unseen to the human eye.

Her name begs to be spoken. A kick to the gut, it is an urge unlike any other. The image of her, two desks in front of me in chemistry for the past few months, is superimposed on the gruesome scene before me. The wisps of hair framing her face, her elegant profile, the way she hunches over her desk while she works. Movement breaks the memory.

The reaper's swirling mixture of light and dark extends toward her face, and a thread of black touches her forehead reverently. The perceived intimacy compels me across snow and blood, my wings bared as a warning to this angelic host.

"Leave her be."

Reapers have no affiliation with Heaven or Hell. They're vessels of Death. Wardens sent to usher souls from this life into the next. I've had limited interaction with others of my kind, but I know about egos. I'm the son of an angel, with a human soul, thanks to the woman who gave me life. One of the Nephilim. In hierarchy alone, I win.

Dropping to my knees, I take in Vivienne's shredded jacket and blood-soaked clothing. Her face matches the snow—pale, deathly. Her lips colorless. Her heart? My hand presses against her chest. The pulse is faint, but it beats. Barely.

The reaper hisses as a ripple shocks the air, shattering the calm. His cloaked form floats back as though pushed by the disturbance. He turns, and his piercing blue eyes hold my gaze. *She is mine, son of angels.* His voice does not speak for human ears. He has no body, no face—only a mist-like outline and blue eyes.

"She isn't dead." My hands rip at her clothing, searching out her injuries.

Her heart beats. He can't kill her. Reapers don't kill. They reap souls once the earthly bodies die, nothing more. I can save her. Grabbing my sweatshirt from where I keep it tucked into my waistband when I fly, I staunch the flow of blood from her wounds. The fabric soaks through immediately. A call to medics won't help. She'll be dead in minutes.

As though he's read my mind, the reaper reaches out once again, straining for her. This is Death. I have no part in it. I barely know Vivienne. She's a classmate, not even a friend. A beautiful girl I've known my entire life, but who has never been impressed by me or my antics.

"Don't take her." The words pour from my lips as the falls pour through the rocks of Cooley Creek. "Can't you spare her? Does she have to die?"

My questions are futile. Reapers don't decide these things. There is a larger plan. We all merely follow it. My fists slam the ground. Why can't I walk away?

*She is special,* the reaper speaks in my mind, soft and low. *Lovely. Her soul was meant for more.*

He rambles like someone in awe. His little, obsessive words click through my head. *I want, I want, I want,* he murmurs. *So special. So different.*

Rage builds within my chest as his chattering continues. Spots flash in my vision, and my stomach hardens as bitterness coats my tongue.

"She is mine!" I shout the statement within my soul and out of my lips.

*No. She is mine, son of angels.*

Low, guttural anger rips from within, snapping my control. My hands burn as my muscles bunch and flex, and the world around us dims, blackness snuffing out the afternoon sun. Shadows grow long, branches creak, and the reaper drifts away once again.

I mock his pitiful presence. "Yes, I *am* the son of an angel. I do not cower before a warden of Death."

"You are a boy," the reaper says aloud, his shroud waving in the wind as the heat consuming my hands creeps up my arms.

The light of a thousand fires burns at the tips of my fingers pressed against Vivienne's wounds. *Heal her.* I call upon an ability I possess, but have never tapped into. My teeth grind in my tight jaw.

The reaper's hisses are nonstop. He is furious. I'm saving his prey, taking his prize. His electric eyes flash as he lowers to the ground and assumes an upright position, hovering above the snow. He remains nothing but spirals of mist, taking the loose shape of the classic specter of Death humans are used to visualizing.

A cold touch shocks my side, and I flinch. *Vivienne's hand.* It slides down my bare ribs, searching for purchase. Her fingers curl around a belt loop of my black jeans as her back arches off the ground. The intensity in my palms grows, and pain contorts Vivienne's features. Her brows draw above her eyes, her mouth forming a voiceless scream as a dribble of blood coats her bottom lip. Her free hand digs into the snow. Her suffering torments me, and yet I hold tight, healing her as she writhes. Her heels scrape against the wet ground as her legs bend and stretch. She's missing one running shoe.

Then it's done.

The light dies. The weak, gray sun reappears.

Vivienne's eyes flutter, offering little glimpses of watery blue nirvana before they close, and her head falls to the side.

With a smug grin, I lift my gaze to the reaper.

*I want her,* he says with his mind, his eyes.

My lip curls. "You can't have her."

*I will.* His black head tilts, a subtle nod, then he's gone.

The forest awakens, the calm of death no longer holding life at a standstill.

My coarse breaths come quickly, my pulse racing as I gather Vivienne close. Leaning over her, I press my lips to the frozen edge of her ear. "It's okay. I've got you. You're safe."

Her heart beats, strong and steady.

My muscles relax as I survey the forest. It's nearly nightfall. The temperature dropped rapidly in the last several minutes. The air is ripe with the scent of the gathering storm. It's a mile, possibly two, north. Tucking my ruined sweatshirt between our bodies, I search the ground for evidence of what transpired here. Her blood is everywhere, but nothing else. The storm will cover the blood from human eyes, although the scent will drive the supernaturals in town crazy. Nothing to be done right now. I need to move Vivienne someplace warm.

Cradling her close, I leap into the air and snap my wings wide. I'll take her to my house, clean her up, and make sure she's okay. I'll figure out my next move after that.

Purchase *Awaken the Soul* at your favorite book retailer.

www.ingramcontent.com/pod-product-compliance
Lightning Source LLC
Chambersburg PA
CBHW052005170626
46808CB00007B/2779